THE INANIMATE WORLD

THE INANIMATE WORLD

Stories
by Robert Strandquist

INDEPENDENT
PUBLISHERS

ANVIL PRESS / VANCOUVER

The Inanimate World

Printed and bound in Canada

Cover design: Rayola Graphic Design
Author photo: Ingrid Rasmussen
Page layout and design by Vancouver Desktop

CANADIAN CATALOGUING IN PUBLICATION DATA

Strandquist, Robert Arthur, 1952–
The inanimate world

ISBN 1-895636-33-7

I. Title
PS8587.T6789152 2001   C813'.6   C00-910952-8
PR9199.3.S8343152 2001

Represented in Canada by the Literary Press Group

Distributed by General Distribution Services

The publisher gratefully acknowledges the financial assistance of the B.C. Arts Council, the Canada Council for the Arts, and the Book Publishing Industry Development Program (BPIDP) for their support of our publishing program.

Anvil Press
Suite 204-A 175 East Broadway,
Vancouver, B.C. V5T 1W2 CANADA
www.anvilpress.com

for Tecla

ACKNOWLEDGMENTS

Earlier versions of some of these stories were published in the following journals:

Thrill Kill *(subTerrain)*, Frank's Friends *(Prairie Fire)*, The Inanimate World *(Canadian Fiction Magazine)*, Real Family *(Grain)*, Deeper Than the World *(Fiddlehead)*, Potential Is Cool Fire *(Prairie Fire)*, Dreaming Is a Relative Thing *(Capilano Review)*.

CONTENTS

THE INANIMATE WORLD

To GET AN IDEA OF THE ROOM'S antiquity, examine the molding around the door—the edges softened by coats of gray and yellow and blue, and eggshell freshly laid—exposed where I bumped it with a speaker cabinet yesterday. And see where the steep roof slices through a corner of the L-shaped room to create a slope in the ceiling and a shorter wall, where behind the tasteful Christmas tree a truncated door conceals Lucille's romance novels and my Castanedas and Steinbecks. Over the fireplace we display our first edition Updikes, antiquarian oddities and a signed *A Spaniard in the Works*. That Francis Rattenbury built the house for his mistress and was murdered in one of the bedroomsg gives the house verve and depth, and adds ambiance to our parties. We feel lucky to have it, the top floor, and we feel blessed indeed to live in Victoria on its sunny promontory by the sea. Lucille has a T-shirt that says *I live here*, a pre-emptive reaction to the pushy operators of horse-drawn tours and the

Queen Elizabeths handing out butterflies and tiny monkey brochures. Lucille is disdainful of the tourists and their flypaper experiences, yet she's employed in the industry herself. It's a paradox not lost on her. Genius is the ability to hold contradictions in the same embrace. I don't know who said that first but Lucille says it often enough. She has a Master of Arts and is a receptionist at the wax museum. Sometimes she'll sit perfectly still as the wary sightseer approaches, not knowing what to expect or sure of what's real. They go into a trance that slows time, and are startled and relieved when she smiles at them. We're all like that, we citizens of the capital, superior to the gaudy visitor and his fat camera. My contribution to the guest list tonight is Elmer and Elvis, students like myself, though younger, expert beer guzzlers who like Johnny Rotten and Ionesco's *Rhinoceros*, though most of the guests are Lucille's friends, writers with day jobs, editors, curators, a professor. And a woman I don't know, who is the most striking individual I have ever seen.

I try to watch her without being obvious, noticing the remarkable effect she has on men, and matter. The chameleon walls blush and armchairs quiver like compass needles. A loose, sandy braid dangles down the swell of her behind, and interesting most of all is that her face isn't pretty, but complex and magnetic. She would have been a gangly stick of a child, unaffected. Maturing, she would have been distressed by her power to turn men into stone. My chance comes when I see her alone and absorbed in one of my e.e. cummings, but something stops me from going over, one too many beer perhaps, though that wouldn't normally stop me. It's that she's reading the book with the tips of her fingers. Her eyes closed.

I get a beer and stand in the hall conversing with my cigarette. Her name, Susan Henry, I learn from another of Lucille's new friends, an "out" socialist and nondrinker, the one who brought the Perrier. I glance around for Elvis, wanting to tell him I found the culprit and that he's pretty much as we speculated: shoulder length curls and a bar mustache that hides a serious lack of imagination. I nod and encourage him to keep talking. Being a rare good listener I make people interesting to themselves. Partway through his story about meeting Lucille he bends over to pick up a cigarette, which he hands to me, apologetically, and I see the one I'm smoking isn't where it was supposed to be. *Did I drop that?* Clownish gravity to cover my drunkenness, I urge him to continue, but he can see that I despise him.

Lucille's and my records are blended, with two of many, and of John Lennon's first solo album three, as I've just discovered, wondering who it belongs to, with its impressed initials that point to a precedent male. Lennon's solo stuff was never uplifting and now that he's dead, it impoverishes, hangs you up. I'm almost tempted to put it on to see the effect, but I'm caught by the pictures, the frightened child Lennon and the unhappy leaning-on-a-woman man, and I wonder why I know more about him than I do about myself. It's been two weeks since the slaying and concussion still rings in our ears. Lucille's best friend, Gillian, stoops beside me and I can smell her workout, her Martha Graham devotion, her lacking dancer's body hanging over my shoulder; tactfully she says, *I love that one too, but maybe we better not play it. I might cry.* What she means is that Lucille might cry, or worse. It was a night like this when news of the killing arrived like a drunk at a children's party. The air became chilly and smelled faintly of garbage, as though the walls had vanished. Someone turned on the TV for confirmation and an excitement began to grow. Loss can be strangely invigorating. Lucille was disgusted with her friends and told them they had to leave, even though it wasn't our party.

We agree on Joni Mitchell and with my graphite brush I drag the slit for dust, which is pretty much mostly human skin, so they say. In spite of my skill at balancing a turntable, and my steady hand, the needle zippers over the first song and halfway through the second. I find Susan Henry leaning on the fridge, chatting in blank verse. I induce her to move the few inches I need to reach in for a beer, plant myself in listening range and nod when I detect a topic. Quite drunk, I watch her finger orbit the rim of her wine glass and listen to the tone.

Waves thrash and withdraw. Gaze into the trough between strokes, see with a painter's eye the emerald serpent, cold and pentimento, the under drawing of hewn blocks like giant steps of lost Atlantis. The curved breakwater points a quarter mile finger, though at what it aims can't be known. Lucille shows me a joint, a question to which I nod. Messed with by the wind, we huddle and blow and I become aware of my thoughts as we stroll towards the light at the end, enjoying the sensation of intelligence, though it doesn't last. Collapsing into anxiety I wonder why I smoke the shit. For some reason it's essential. It strips from reality its covering of sentimental aggravations and comfortable blindness, letting you see more clearly a deeper blindness, exhilarating and nightmarish. Steadily the grey range across the strait and the grim whitecaps march in.

Have we decided then? She asks.

Yes, I say, *John,* trying to wrench myself out of the anodyne gloom. We are not alone out here and I'm forced to adjust my mask. I study them study me, a trespasser in their thoughts. The concrete base of the light provides a poor shelter. The wind off the end of the jetty clashes with the outgoing tide over the privilege of being first, or last.

And if it's a girl, Joni, I say, as I discover my nose bleeding, which I dab with the balled up tissue I find in my pocket.

The idea of having a child with Lucille was sexy until it exploded like a suicide bomber into untenable reality. But acceptance poured into the crater and my doubts became transparencies, adding up to a kind of skin. But I shouldn't have smoked that joint; cold wisdom returns: *Will I be able to keep writing my futile poetry?* And my not-yet-ex-wife, how will it sit with her and my first-born? Is it a betrayal to them? If it is should I care? I swore I'd never be like my father and yet who am I? I'm thinking too much. Anticipating baby packs and diapers alarms me. I don't want to be one of those lugs you see in the supermarket. A new father is a pack animal. Fear breaks over me. I have barely self-esteem to get myself through a day let alone two of us.

John or Joni it is, I say, bravely going on fumes, just needing definition from Lucille, some determination.

If you decide we keep it, she says, stopping to look into my face, something I realize she doesn't often do.

I thought it was decided, I say.

I want you to decide, she says.

Me? You want me to decide? I'm shocked and I feel betrayed. *Why?*

I want you to be sure that this is what you want.

But sometimes what I want isn't what I want, I try to explain.

You'd better figure it out.

Damn it, I gently say, meaning that only a woman has those tools, or a soldier, and I'm only a skillful fool that maneuvered himself to no choice. Please don't take that away.

Twist and turn through neighbourhoods ablaze with children, race along like a couple of mice on a greeting card, quiet mice, sad mice. It's early December and a twelve-mile journey in my cartoon blue vw Beetle that leaks carbon monoxide through the heating vents to our new place at Lost Lake. The abortion sits between us like an extortionist; our objectivity withers. On the outskirts of the city we stop at the IGA and push it around in a shopping cart; and in Brentwood we go to the liquor store for beer and wine and at the last corner, on the edge of forest that time forgot, I buy cigarettes and remember to get plenty of ice. Gliding past the few neighbours, we pull up on our designated patch and step into the quiet air, smiling at each other. This is good, the country is a balm to our mutual detachment; though late at night when local clatter settles, the city burbles clearly in the distance, not escaped at all but only shelved. Lucille fills bowls with snacks and I stack the beer in the fridge. She dresses like a vamp and I put on my lumberjack shirt. Among the regulars tonight the personal friend of a Nobel laureate is coming and a woman who was briefly lovers with Trudeau. It's my job to keep fire in the grate. And to not drink too much.

Though I am watching for her, I don't see Susan Henry arrive. She just materializes a piece at a time, first her voice, then her body a few minutes later. I work a nice dry piece of cherry into the flame. It was one of our reasons for moving, a real hearth, making all the difference to our imperturbable love. I get some beer and head out under the deck where Elmer and Elvis are hovering and give them each one, leaving two for me, one which I down and the other drink quickly.

She's here, I tell them.

This party reminds me of Pinter, Elmer says.

There's no one, says Elvis, spraying beer, *I repeat, no one, not in this country at any rate, who knows more about the Pinter pause than I do.* Pausing, he finishes, *Seriously.*

Three-point-two seconds, Elmer says.

I want female companionship, so I hunt down Gillian and take her to the yard to see my newly sprouted pot plant. But the porch light doesn't reach that far so we go up on the landlord's deck and stare at the black lake. I banter easily, surprising myself with unlocking, like an actor on speed, these past grim months parting for this unconcerned nonsense. My hand on the hard small of her back, I show her around the suite and steer her to the unfinished part of the basement to show her the old furnace with its Shiva robot arms. And I start kissing her. She moves backwards to the wall pulling me with her, elevating her centre of gravity by standing on ductwork. Unfurling my kite string she lifts me up to her rain, where I tremble and thunder and she contracts and expands, satisfying the both of us well and quick.

To cheat on a wife is one thing, but to betray a girl-friend . . . . Husbands who do it follow a biological thread, behaving in a manner consistent with nature. They obey a higher nagging and act out of a sense of responsibility, a solemn doom, protecting their families from the harsher expressions of selection, defusing oblivion's need to dance. But to cheat on a girlfriend breaks a whole other ethic involving higher promises and delicate compromises with trust, and is proof you will never be more than what you are. My thoughts generate cold. Intellectual and guilty, I splash down a beer to loosen the feeling, more complicated than that, ranging to panic. I pick at the stubby bottle's label, tearing away small strips. Lucille comes over, touching bases. She doesn't believe me when I tell her I'm having a good time. She kindly and firmly asks me to not drink anymore, this being where I'm supposed to surrender to better judgement. But I hate her for pretending everything's okay.

Susan Henry comes outside and wanders through the garden down to the tiny dock that stepping onto sends goose bumps over the lake. I'd follow her and be boyishly charming. I would, but I feel like dirt. I lean against the linden tree and stare at her hourglass figure and see how much of my soul has turned to sand.

I'm meeting Lucille for lunch and she's late. The clock above the bar says quarter after. We've been marking the days in mental ink and today she's supposed to get her test results. Why do beer parlours smell so bad? I go outside and lean on the fence. Examining my mood, I find impatience. Cranky is not the face I need her to see right now. She appears at the other end of the block, but I can't read her. She exudes quixotic self-confidence, same as usual. I meet her at the corner and we go down a lane so I can light up a joint.

Have you heard? I don't need to ask. I hold down a toke.

No, she says.

I pose the joint but she declines.

There's something you should know. She stops me with a hard compassionate look. *It wasn't the first abortion and I have no intention of having another.*

It was your idea to give me the choice . . . I say, foolishly. We stop beside a patch of desert flowers in a vacant lot.

It was stupid to name it first.

We walk in silence for a while. It's so much easier accepting a thing than trying to deal with it. We get sandwiches from a take-out and eat walking back to the wax museum.

On her desk is a message to call her doctor. I stand aside to make room for a few couples bumping the counter. She holds them off with a raised hand when someone starts speaking to her on the line. They look at each other with irritated patience, jingling radioactive coins over their gene pools. Putting the receiver down Lucille catches her breath, and speaking to them not me, says, *I'm pregnant.* She wants witnesses, to help fix the fetus in her, so nature won't dislodge it, so I can't.

I'll pick you up at five, I tell her. She smiles, in love with herself again.

I decide to go through the gallery. I love Queen Victoria's face. Though she won't look directly back, she is flattered. Ugly women aren't ugly at all, but lovers incognito, their uncompromising lusts meant to attract men with x-ray vision and loose egos. Einstein here, whose eyes I want to touch to see if he blinks, is an even better listener than me. If it takes the greatest thinker in history to see your genius, is that a good thing or a bad thing? Lucille pregnant, I feel barenaked and light as crepe, the baby an orthotic for my heart; its recognizable imperative of burden is at least something, rails through the flux and flounder of my moods. My sins are absorbed by the figures, it's what they breathe, what nourishes them, gives them their pallor. I come to the dungeon and see the torture of wax men still goes on to this day. Deplorable and hokey, the two sides of the meat, solar powered and born to die, which makes everything frivolous and revelations bitter. If people would just stop striving so hard for peace there would be no wars. I walk home with new muscle, censor my thoughts with a joint.

I'm face down on a table while my doctor sprays aerosol Novocain on a cyst on my neck. When it became infected, young Frankenstein tried to treat it with oral antibiotics. I went in yesterday afternoon much worse, and a disconcerting alarm registered on his blank chart face. *This is going to be a bit uncomfortable,* he says, weighing the lance in his fingers, his voice uneasy. I don't feel anything at first, a tentative cut, an eerie silence. But then he uses his thumbs to squeeze out the puss and pushes me down to molten core, where I recite poltergeist and flail. That he's capable of causing such suffering ravages him by its unwelcome pleasure. Flustered, he leaves as soon as the procedure is done. My head spins like a gyroscope on a wire and my heart has a dream of falling. Standing before me is Lucille's doctor. Where am I? Did anyone else survive? Has he dropped in to visit? Why does that sound so stupid? Lucille has miscarried. She's one corridor over. I put on my shirt and wander in a daze until I find her, pale and still. I'm saddened by her luck and anesthetized by familiar loss. Redemption would have been too much of a burden anyway. Lucille stares past me. She has that look. The inanimate world.

Elvis keeps his thermostat set at "abandoned building." A stack of empty beer cans can topple if you don't hold it when you're in his fridge, which he demonstrates for us, handing us a cold one. I look around for a place to sit but the couch is scaly with textbooks and laundry. He brought us up to hear the new stereo his student loan bought him, on which he plays nothing but hardcore punk, which makes the room even colder. Its churning chaos is like a skinned animal, all tendon and rage.

What's the point of playing that kind of music on such a nice system? I ask him.

He gives me a blank stare and smiles. He thinks I'm kidding.

It would be better on a cheap one, I say, unintentionally shooting down his taste in music, his ignorance of form, his ability to make choices.

Was Hamlet really indecisive or just sadistic? Elmer asks, to ease the tension. *A brilliant man doesn't belong to other men,* says Elvis morosely. *If Shakespeare was so precise how come no one can agree on what he was talking about? Me. He layered opposites on opposites,* Elvis. *So he only appears insane? Elmer. He's dead, like the rest of us,* I say.

Elvis turns on me, nearly shouting, *He hath born me on his back a thousand times, alas!*

Lucille is having a party tonight that I wasn't invited to, showing off her new husband, a well-known naturalist credited with uncovering the last lost tribe of the Amazon. He just hiked into the wax museum one afternoon and there was the motionless Lucille. Apparently he'd never seen anything so beautiful.

I'm kneeling over Elvis' turntable with a large pair of pliers intending to replace the cartridge with another he claims is designed for punk. He was going to have a technician do it but I insist on saving him some money, to make up for the insults. He stands over me in the watery light, his anxiety getting to me. When I've gotten the original cartridge amputated and disconnected, I stop.

Don't they ever heat this fucking place? I ask.

You're not stopping?

I'm afraid of wrecking it.

What about my music?

You can't seriously call that music.

What would you call it?

Graffiti.

Asshole.

Standing in the lane I listen to laughter and music radiating from Lucille's top-floor windows. We talked about staying together when she found this place. It was tempting for us to try again, talking about the abandonment of hope and us leading semi-separate lives together. In the huge apartment we could each have had a study, one being unpleasantly large and overlooking road hockey, while the other had a hardwood floor and windows on three sides. A craving for a beer and vaguer urgencies around Lucille's friends pulls me up. I greet a few faces and listen to the surf sound of many conversations, where *big island* bobs like a bleach bottle, Lucille having earned a standing invitation to use the house's owners' condo in Kona. Our discussion about staying together centred on who got the good study, an idea Lucille found slightly repugnant, though she wouldn't relent either. So I settled in a cheap room around my boxes of records and books and she went out and married the first Ph.D. off the boat. She's in the crowded big room, happy as a toucan. I don't know what I expected him to be like, at least magnetic and articulate, but her groom, I realize, standing off to the side, is at a loss for words.

I return to the kitchen where someone is passing a joint around. After I've had a hit and offered it back I realize no one is paying attention so I squeeze it dead and pocket it. No beer in the fridge but bottles of wine everywhere. I kidnap a litre of Kressman and take my leave just as Susan Henry is coming up the stairs. She smiles at me. But voices in the kitchen tell me I'm being pursued by the owner of the wine and all I can do is nod, escape.

I'm sitting in the last row of folding chairs, easiest to escape from should I decide to bolt before they do the serenity prayer. I'm twenty-five minutes early having forgotten this meeting starts at eight-thirty instead of eight like most of them. Eagerness blows into the room with members shucking their burdens at the door and scanning the room for their supporters. A tough chick in leopard skin tights sits down in my row, between an old man and a fine-boned rich girl. I'm wondering how identity chooses one person over another. It's your weakest link, your name, the sack you're born in and what they'll carry you out with. It's better to have an alias, several of them, free from baptisms and brass plates. And if you can't do that, admit to a room full of people that you're an alcoholic.

Someone says a few words of welcome. Others read routine steps and promises, comforting in their imperfections. The unskilled newcomers and the farthest fallen are who I come for, their clanking tirades and hopeless hope, its blunt assurance of liberation. But the first speaker is an old hand whose terrors he's honed into a landscape of generalities. This is not helping. Next up is a thirty-year chippee who tells a convoluted patronizing parable. I want it to end and glance towards the exit. The chair asks, *Does anybody need to share?* I should, and occasionally do, but my story involves too much overwriting in empty rooms, and I can see their eyes glaze over when I tell it and their skin soften under the lights. I was walking on Jericho Beach this morning, with acrid Vancouver dampness in my craw, searching English Bay for the inspiration I believe it owes me, when I saw Susan Henry coming down the path the other way. Even though she's changed, I recognized her objective eyes do their familiar, succinct double-take on me. It was cool and windy and the waves were running at the shore to the end of their chains. She and her companion leaned into each other's voices, worn smooth under the ceaseless rolling. And it gave me a lift to see her, but soon after brought me down hard and I wanted to get drunk. The suddenly ending meeting has cut off my escape, chairs are being scraped aside and a circle of bodies forms, all around the mulberry bush . . . I hate this, holding hands. The prayer I've memorized, *God, grant me the serenity to accept the things I cannot change . . .*

California rolls, egg rolls, chicken wingettes and teriyaki salmon; there are bean salads, potato salads, Caesar salad, four different breads, including the French loaf I brought, and a quarter pound of garlic butter. There are crackers with exotic dips, oysters on the half shell and Rice Crispy squares, Nanaimo bars and a box of chocolates. Entrees, hors d'oeuvres and desserts, all laid out at once, so democratic, so fattening. I make my way around the table, sampling and filling my plate, and then make for an empty chair. Parties are sober torture and I don't know a soul. The friends I'm supposed to meet are fashionably late, which I always forget to be. I make my way through a hatch of women, clustered around the kitchen entrance, and locate my non-alcoholic beverage. Unopened among more seductive bottles, I pour myself a glass. Then she walks in and for a second something is naked between us, terrifying the both of us with its touching disregard for the passing of time.

To throw something on it she says, *We've been running into each other at parties for years, haven't we?* Brilliantly obtuse by stating the obvious.

And I say, *Yes we have*, sharing this with her, making contact.

You know Lucille . . .

Yes, I tell her, awed by how arbitrary the meanings we assign things are.

Isn't that great about her having twins again?

Yes . . . indeed, I say, though I don't know anything, and before I can think of something to hold her, she escapes to the other room.

I follow with my fruit juice and find a chair where I can keep an eye on her. When I look more closely I

don't understand why I recognize her, so different
from memory she is. I organize a few conversations in
my head, how Vancouver compares with Victoria,
Lucille's children. But before I can approach her, something comes into the room, a shockwave or a trapped
bird, I'm not sure which, and hard rumour becomes
soft fact, *Princess Diana is what?* Somebody turns on the
TV, and so much for talk.

Later, conversation returns to original sin, and I'm
back to grazing at the table when Susan Henry appears
beside me, picking up a grape and a cube of cheese, and
offering me the weakest of smiles, which I try and cap-
ture with clumsy words. *You must be tired after all this,* I
say, *I know I am.* For a heartbeat she blushes. Now she
has to say something real. No small talk exists between
us. But the hostess appears and draws her away, Susan
Henry, reluctantly eager, my poor fugitive breathless
me.

COLLECTING SHADOWS

1   DREAMING IS A RELATIVE THING

O N THE LIP OF THE GREAT PLAINS north of Saskatoon and east of Love a man is standing on the CN mainline gauging the temperature by counting ties. Yesterday he got to twenty, but now they swim together in a blur at fifteen. It's hotter today. A red automobile appears on the concurrent road as it does every morning pulling its chute of dust in the direction of town. Of his dream last night he retains nothing. He doesn't remember dreams, but knows them by their brood, the quixotic yearnings and unfathomable moods.

He lays a slice of sweating meat by-product on stiff bread and fills a tumbler with tap water. The refrigerator is dust. He sits in the yard trying to do some work under the parasol of his spastic table, his aluminum chair creaking under his solemn features. His pen feels heavy as an oar, and his distracted thoughts make prints on the river, impermanent and unnecessary; on his river, which he sold cheap, that floods the rooms of his memory and carries it away, the writing he sacrificed everything for. He makes the pen write: *The children have no faces and the dogs lick themselves because they can; men are lost without precious cold war* . . . He crumples it up and tosses it to the ground. With no wind or rain your mediocrity stays where you drop it.

At midnight the westbound freight rushes past, creating a mild shaking in the ground and a small breeze that Doug can feel if he stands close enough to the hammering wheels. It's the only moving air. Boxcars sway and tankers have *flammable* stenciled on their sides, or *inflammable*. Standing closer, his hair rustles and fear expands loosely in his gut, giving him a measure of peace.

He stands in the bright driveway, moving his toes. The ball of paper he threw there centuries ago hasn't moved. The sun is directly overhead and crickets have surrounded him with their dry fiddling. He wants to look at one to see if they have features besides this monotonous countdown, but he's incapable of the subtlety of movement required.

He needs to talk; to begin to accept this place, he needs to tell someone how much he hates it. To share his curse like bread would be incredible. He trudges up the road to a farmhouse on the hill where he thought he saw puffs of cigarette smoke. But the place is rented by wind; and anyway, people treat honesty like a slap in the face.

In the middle of the night how cool the rails are compared with the unavoidable heat. He places his cheeks and temples on the iron moonlight; holding his sweaty hair back he chills his neck and his arms and wrists. He stares at the sky and absorbs what he can of it from the steel.

Falling asleep he dreams about the air raid siren on the hill above Hume Elementary, perched on a pole like a specimen from the fossil record, a crude arthropod painted battleship gray. They tested it regularly, giving interrupted bursts like a cat's horny growl, and showed films about living in teepees made from doors, and waiting out the black snow under a dome of branches and twigs. He's dreaming about trains when the starved sun crawls on his face; and with a yelp of pure terror he scrambles off the tracks. But there is only silence and his crackling luck and in his pants the ecstasy of risk. His hands were severed in the dream and it bothers him for the rest of the day, though for some reason writing becomes possible. He tosses off a poem and settles into revisions, happy for a few hours in the gather of his focus. He drinks warm beer and fleshes it out and then drinks more beer and pares it back until the poem is cold and the beer pissed away.

At midnight he's waiting for the train. It comes out of the east a few minutes ahead of itself and is only briefly material before him where he can actually touch it, just a matter of seconds really and he's watching after it, a memory of an echo, a memory of a memory.

He wakes up on the ground entangled in the chair. The sky is a bell that won't stop ringing. He takes a couple of Tylenol. Later he makes coffee and sits down to imagine a cigarette. Tunneling home from the west comes the red car. The woman driving has long unaffected brown hair. Glancing off him she accelerates up the river of dust and slips like a drop of blood over the wavering top.

At midnight he kisses the rails and lies between them. He is a pool of adrenaline reflecting the stars. *That taste, what is it?* Terror holds him, thunder sings, and he coos like a baby woven into its mother's arms.

A two-mile hike into Love down the tracks that cut diagonally across the rectangles and gridlines of local nature. In the laundromat he buys a machine Coke and drinks it down. In the bar he picks up a case of beer and at the grocery store a bottle of Black Label rye, a couple dozen wieners, a handful of chocolate bars and a pound of coffee. He gives in to cigarettes and smokes one on the laundromat steps. Listening to the spin cycle, he's held up by the gravity of practical matters. That neither of the dryers work he loses two quarters finding out.

Getting home he drops everything to the floor and stands in the shower with his clothes on. Wet laundry hangs over a railing and on withdrawing nails in the unpainted siding. The chocolate bars are liquid and the beer is hot. He soaks himself again and stands outside to evaporate.

He lights a smoke and stares off into himself, half the

cigarette burning down before he takes another drag.
Uncanny addictions return to the stream that spawned
them. An *S* in the dust moves past him and he traps it
under foot. Picking it up, the garter snake coils around
his hand, reminding him of the spontaneous cruelty of
children. How long does it take to drown a snake? You
can't ever know because it outlasts innocence. His fingers smell of reptile even after he's washed.

In a dream he ties a red balloon to a grass snake. He
can see it out there on the hillside, sometimes not moving for days then appearing on the other side of the
tracks. He fastens a blue balloon to a king snake and
watches it move steadily towards the horizon and dis-
appear. To a yellow one he ties a small rattler, which
lifts into the air above the house and drifts towards the
hill. It will eat birds and black cherries from unreachable
branches and come down when it's good and heavy; a
snake that understands more than other snakes, that will
want to kill him for it.

Smoking in the red brick shade of the hospital he
feels guilty as hell trying to remember when he was last
here. A balloon floats above the water tower. Grinding
out his filter he goes through the aquarium-glass doors
into cool chemical air.

In the years immediately following the catastrophe,
after his mother died, the only woman *either* of them had
ever loved, the relationship between father and son was
by necessity improved, though it wasn't automatic, a
loose weave of mixed signals and ambivalent loyalties. It

lasted until the old man moved back to Love. Caring for his aging parents was easier. Doubtful emotion mattered less than the daily penance of duty. And he was only an hour's drive from the cemetery. By the time his parents were gone his Parkinson's had advanced and Doug was struck by an inspiration to follow his noble lead. He impaled himself on the idea that he had something to fix and decided it was an opportunity to write a book. When he stepped off the bus with his spent one-way ticket in hand, all assets liquid, there it was to greet him, the familiar bedrock of the old man's indifference. He had encouraged him to come. Or had he? He said things he thought his children wanted to hear, a trick he learned after their mother died, the only way he knew to hold them.

He sits with his back to the door watching commercials. Removing his hearing aid he scratches a toothpick in his ear, the earphone dangling near the pickup produces feedback. He coughs in a deliberate precise way to get at the same bottomless itch, and Doug can't go any closer.

He stands in the shower with a glass of whisky. Then he takes up his pen and finds himself lost. He never believed it, that a blank sheet of paper was death to inspiration. But it's true, and the pen feels heavy as a woman's leg. A child steps out of the wheat field at the foot of the driveway. Picking up a handful of road she throws it at him and then runs back into the waves.

He writes, *Hard soft river, the giant ships are filled with silence, cautious as an hour hand. He just stepped out his door to watch them.* He smokes deliberately, making rings in the stillness, the haloes of devoured angels. He took his rowboat to the quay in the afternoons for coffee. He slept through the night on the river's cool skin.

At midnight he's sitting between the tracks. Maybe he's dreaming. Maybe dreaming is a relative thing. A yellow balloon floats down with its snake bloated from crows and crucifixes. It opens wide and swallows him wet dream first.

He awakes in a shroud, appalled they've buried him alive, terrified to know there is only ego after death and what it's like to be rock. He can see the living through a pinhole though they're upside down and the universe isn't expanding, after all. There was no big bang, no birth of fingertips. A face appears and words cluster for naming, Cactus and Stone, and what's that hanging there? A tear, a single mirroring crushing sea. And Doug comes back into the cold clattering room.

A nurse pushes him to the garden and parks him beside the ashtray. She puts a cigarette in his mouth and holds a flame on her thumb. When she puts the cigarette to his lips her fingers touch. He steals these caresses, careful not to reveal what they are, listening to her voice, her stories about Jesus and Mary.

If Dougy's dad isn't home by Friday afternoon it usually means he won't be for the weekend. From the raspberry bush he studies the kitchen window. That's where he'd be, at the hostage table, aligning everything to himself. But it's empty. He goes up the steps at the side of the garage with his fingers crossed and yes, the Plymouth isn't there. He goes into the kitchen where Mum has dough rising in bread pans. *Your dad's up north and he won't be back until next weekend.* She deep-fries strips of it, dough gods, which they smear with jam and honey.

In bed the furnace motor lulls him to the edge of sleep and then flutters off. In the naked silence he hears a descending whistle coming louder and closer, the movie sound of a falling bomb, and terror mushrooms inside him, rupturing his flow, exposing the nightmare workings. But it was a truck on the highway, the wind blowing across a mirror.

II   POTENTIAL IS COOL FIRE

DOUGY IS WAITING FOR WORLD WAR III. Everyone is waiting for World War III. It's a sunny and cool October day. He's building roads in the garden. While neighbours mutter over fences, bus mechanics at the high school huddle over rags. Dougy is alone but not alone. World War III is his friend. It has the voice of Cronkite and a cellophane skin. Everything makes sense: the air raid siren above the school, the rough smooth dream. The waiting. World War III waits with him. The world hangs below, quivering, ready to drop.

Though as the day fills up with nods of sleep he fears nothing is going to happen. Familiar promises. He's cranky and tired.

His dream is a mass of swirling mixing grey and dark grey, characters without shape, images without cognition, convecting souls, blends of nausea, decaying echo. He wakes slowly in a swamp with cold edges, but snuggles back out on his warm raft, to womb dreams, fish consciousness, turtles flying backwards. But he keeps waking up and shivering in the shallow grave his wet bed makes.

The teacher kneels beside him to answer his how a jet works question, explaining that burning gas creates forward thrust. *Yah but how?* The teacher explains, *It burns so hot that thrust is the outcome.* Dougy says, *That doesn't explain it.* The teacher says, *It's just basic physics.*

The desolate hours of school must be filled. There are erasers to carve, rulers to measure the parts of the body, rubber cement for rolling into snot, paper clips for unbending and rebending. All his pencils are nubs and all his pens hard toffee. He spends time deepening a hole he's carved into the pressboard desktop with his compass needle. He wedges a .22 calibre blank into the hole and tries to pry it open. He wants to see gunpowder. How can something have so much potential? Hold the cartridge to your lips and feel it. Potential is cool fire. Put it in your mouth, taste your hands, and if you suck, coal and urine. The teacher says: *Dougy are you eating candy?* He swallows. *Cough drop,* he says. Cool fire tingles. If it went off there'd be no scar, no point of entry. Impressive. He rescues it from number two.

It's Saturday afternoon. Dougy and Donny are stuck cleaning the basement on a day their friends are battling the kids from over the hill, mud war paint, slingshots, BB guns. It's probably too late. They should have been there two hours ago. Heckle and Jeckle come down the stairs for another inspection. It's a game with private rules. The boys stare at each other; injustice is so sickly sweet. They idly push the broom around for another half century. *Supper will be ready soon, so don't go too far,* Mum frees them. They climb the maple in the backyard and scan the neighbourhood for white feathers, Dad's broad back visible in the kitchen window.

The teacher's voice is slowing and Dougy is unaware of any subject. Working away on his blank he's oblivious of the classroom. Pushing the compass point into the puckered brass, the teacher's words are a lullaby in a foreign language. He pushes and twists and it goes off smashing his thumb and melting half his nail away. The class wakes up, heads turn to scorn. The shaken teacher asks what it was, did he know he could have hurt the girls in the desks in front of him? It was just a blank, he pleads. The injured lesson resumes and his thumb throbs and his blood roars.

On the last day of grade five, the class shortly to be dismissed early, the teacher handing out report cards announces: *All of you passed the year except Dougy, who is going to be repeating.* He is excited; it fits. This is the wrong feeling, he knows, but can't help himself. Running home with the news he tries to look sad, but Mum's as defeated and just as relieved. They expect him to do better next year. It's all going to make perfect sense the second time.

Lego pieces glued back to back with gunpowder in the cavity and a firecracker fuse jutting from a crack. When he lights it in a vacant lot it doesn't explode but flames geyser, so he builds another one with a smaller hole, which jumps around like a wounded bird. For an explosion he needs to seal the hole utterly, a problem to solve during the hours of test-signal hum, sketching ideas on the backs of his notebooks. Experimenting with his eraser achieves his first success, cutting it in half and running a fuse between the reunited pieces, which seams up tight after the fuse burns through. He mounts this under the lid of a jar that has a film of gas in it and sets it off at the dump, caught in the cheek by a carrot of glass, one sticky drop.

   Forehead resting on his arm on his desk, he aims his compass extended like a diver at a spot on the wooden floor. He's supposed to be reading with all the quiet others. He pulls it out and drops it again. This is better than reading, letting his mind drift wherever it wants. If you put a hole in an H-bomb would it jet? There's a gentle tap on his shoulder and he sits up into a heavy book the teacher brings down on his head.

It must have just happened, the window is dark. He shifts to where the sheets are dry, at the foot of the bed. Mum has gone with his Dad to Spokane for ten days. When Dougy wets the bed, which is every night, the babysitter tells him he doesn't love his mother, and she puts his lunch on the floor by the back door.

He fills a dense cardboard tube with the powder of bullets pried open with his teeth. A wire frame holds the ends on and instead of a fuse he uses a blank. The trigger mechanism is gravity. A finishing nail functions as the hammer, set to strike the face dead centre. Painted silver and quickened with badminton feathers, he takes it to the roof of the school, where he peers over the edge at the gym door landing. Insubstantial as a bird and balanced like a dart, it has potential, though he has no idea how much, a large firecracker or a small A-bomb. He can think no thought to prevent him going through with it, even considering the possibility of blowing the gym door off and the science of disgrace. He sets it on the air and it sails straight and true. But nothing comes of it. He fiddles with it, tossing it at walls trying to figure out what he did wrong.

He puts it in his desk where it gets ingested by books, cough drop wrappers, and foil peelings. Dougy is lost in distraction with the girl in the next row two seats down. She's strange and has fist eyes and smells like oranges. It takes his mind off the rat-trap desk and muffles the hypnotist's drone. Everyday he takes her up to the reservoir in his mind where they squeeze each other's fruit.

Circling the bus station Mom runs the stop sign. She's gawking at the damaged walls. *Freedomites,* she says, precisely and carefully and drives around the block for another run at the sign and another look. The post office has a guard full-time, and so does city hall. The dams on the river and the transmission towers on the main lake all have guards. Who would have thought the bus depot?

With a long fingernail he digs dead skin from his scalp, mining sand and undiscovered minerals. It's gratifying, conducive to thought. With his other hand a wild cherry cough drop goes into his mouth. He sucks it half away and adds a licorice one. By some loophole in the scheme of things you're allowed to eat cough candies in school. He digs too deep, a nerve. He starts on a less mined area and decides to try two licorice and two menthol at the same time.

The H-bomb was first detonated in 1952. He perks up; he was born that year. *It was tested on the Eniwetok Atoll,* the teacher solemnly brags.

There's a picture of Dad with a newborn in his arms. The fedora makes it look like an old movie. Was he thinking about the H-bomb, that it had just been tested? Something was bothering him.

The rough smooth dream is sickly damp like flu, delirious and vague, with rivers of magnetism, lakes of nothing, a consciousness not his in pursuit. There is a rubber sheet under the real one. This is supposed to be an improvement. But now he wakes every morning nearly drowned.

It's the last day of school already. They watch a film about water birds and the teacher passes out report cards. *All of you passed this year. I'm pleased,* she says, staring through Dougy with moving blindness. Cleaning out his desk he finds the forgotten experiment. He strikes the plunger a few times and then peels the layers of cardboard until powder spills on the floor and a sweet odour rises from under his feet, the teacher becoming pale.

Sunday they drive south following the river, counting the dams. They crank down the windows to vacuum out the moods and the mistrust and they stop for penny candies and pull off the road so Larry can cast into the river at this spot where he once caught a rainbow trout. Turning off the highway onto gravel, they seal the windows tight and close the vents, though a fine dust you can taste hangs in the air and coats the dash. They drive into Crestova, what's left of it after the protest fires. Doukhobour farms reduced to charcoal drawings. It's hard to fathom the terrorism of barenaked old women. Dougy asks his dad what they would have used to start the fires and he gets an answer to a different question, *It was hot enough to melt glass.* Heading for home at dusk they play the running out of gas game, the car sputtering and jerking, everybody grinning.

From bed Dougy stares at the strip of light under the

door. From the kitchen comes the unintelligible and hypnotic exchange, the business of being, muffled by walls and whisky. He listens to the cadence, the distant drumming.

Dougy is aware of being asleep, and he's afraid of sleep. His thoughts struggle against his body's paralysis, sending urges up the wires, but it's like yelling at a dead dog. He goes into the dark living room exhausted. He stares out at the empty lighted street where a transformer somewhere hums.

III   THE INVISIBLE MAN

THE INTRAVENOUS is a patient stainless steel man. Though who knows what he's thinking, holding up that bag of fluid not entirely dispassionately? His bones are cool but you can see variations in the clockwork pulse as the nurse comes and goes in mortuary white and when Doug detaches the receptacle that irrigates his empty blood. Down the tube goes the liquid into a clear cylindrical reservoir where it drips, body language revealed, the inanimate world's lust for humanity, the rhythm of the will of matter. It winds once around the night rail and across half the length of the bed where it wets onto the sheets. Doug doesn't want their products, their serums; he doesn't know what's in them and he doesn't want to know. It's the orderly's private smile, and the sheer stupidity of God.

Reinserting the male into the female receptor on his wrist, pulling the blanket over the wet spot, he always knows when she's coming, the general nurse and variations on the theme. He watches her elbow face crumple and stretch as she inspects the mechanisms in a ritual of looking without seeing, touching dials without turning them, hoping for the best.

They don't know why he keeps losing weight, or understand each others' version of what they thought they were doing. They struggle with connotations and count each other's fingers. Polite to empty beds, they consult regularly with shiny surfaces. And when *He* comes by making small rounds and rocking on His heels, He asks, *How are we doing today?* And Doug turns to the wall because he can't think of any reason not to.

Another day the nurse has piglet hands with a wedding band so tight he expects her to bleed. *Time for your sponge bath,* she says, meaning: *Time for bed 2 in room 104.* But Doug has an erection and it stands there like a gopher until she bats it with her pencil. She washes him with a cold cloth and he notices how lack of nourishment is excavating his bones, making his ribs countable and his knees clay. Soon he'll be withered down to a single conscious choice. Cactus and Stone will make his way from extended care with another tear and Doug will be visible again.

Polished halls gleam like still water behind a dam. Barreling him through the valley of shrunken apples, around trays on wheels and a housekeeping cart where an idle intravenous contemplates chloral bleach and imagines higher callings, this adaptation of nurse is happiest when she's mad and right when she's wrong, and parks him in the lounge by an old woman who has on her tray the whole range of meds from capsules of baboon blood to tablets of stone. The baby-talking nurse moves her water glass a millimetre closer encouraging the intelligent tree root to smile and pretend she's stupid. She'd have no qualms about killing the nurse. You can see it in her eyes, her life compressed to inevitability and possessed of the priorities of gods.

By necessity, he maneuvers his arm crane-like with its guy wires and pulleys and picks up one of her bright pills, rolling it in his fingers until the logo wears off. Though he tries he can't get it to his mouth. The old woman moves close, takes the pill and puts it between his lips, and with another one alive in her salty fingers she waits for him to blink. She feeds him all of them as he watches her gathering skin. He pushes with his good leg into the hall, backwards in circles until he gets the hang of it, through the doors and outside. A mail truck pulls up and the driver runs in the side entrance. Doug works his way over to the shade at the back of the truck feeling his anxieties evaporate in the placebo of certain doom. The truck curtseys when the driver steps back into the cab and starts it up, the engine chafing against the break, his waybill reading. A blaring horn swamps Doug in headache as a car pulls up beside him, rocking on its shocks as the mail truck backs into it. The furious mail driver encounters nurse Joanne who turns his rage to shame and leaves him standing in the parking lot with a pocket Bible. She puts Doug back in the lounge beside a rotting man playing solitaire with his cards face down. Doug lifts a bottle of cleaning solution from the cart. The gnarly old woman nods. He drinks it down and is shortly swimming in chaos, passing out when hairy arms shove a tube down his throat.

Curious, but knowing his place, Cactus and Stone won't come any closer than the door. Doug is the Doctor's experiment now. Dr.'s Jekyll and Frankenstein, they understand each other of course; it's not easy being a creator. Their promising monsters ransack villages and bring shame to the name. Remember King Kong's confusion and the hunchback's surprise, their wrenching epiphany when they had a glimmer of self- knowledge? This is when they're always brought down, the moment of being most human. Doug starts to cry, desperately fighting it so Cactus and Stone won't be scared off, but it's too late. The Doctor stands beside his bed discovering the intravenous unplugged. He spins the tube in his fingers as he stares at the back of Doug's head. He sniffles and puts it back where he found it. After that, Doug starts leaving it in.

When they take the casts off his arms it feels like amputation. He loses most of his hands, the automatic-as-breathing ones that wound him up and gave his pendulum a nudge; and Joanne's cool marble sculpted by the Master, which he defrauded of kisses. His own claws are frail and clammy, making him swear off cigarettes. A hundred and seventy-seven stitches run over his body like a map of the Grand Trunk and Northern. His left leg in a cast is all that holds him in blessed injury.

Under his own steam, his bony locomotion, he explores the hospital corridors, their alcoves and closets, careful to avoid certain areas. Simple, ordinary free will, it's wonderful, all the decisions about which way to turn. He unearths possessions of the dead, boxes of books and paintings of waves, disintegrating in the unheated storage room; and piles of clothes, a stack of bricks, and at least two riding mowers. Going out the wrong door finds him in extended care, staring at a pair of shoes, terrible collapsed shoes, for some reason unmistakable. And he's a child again sitting on the sofa watching Championship Wrestling, his dad sprawled in his armchair, his big black shoes lay beside the hassock. Dougy can't tell if the wrestling is real, and nobody else can either. They can't admit they don't know, not even the wrestlers. Doug knows it's madness to ask his dad for money. He'll get nosy and demand a justification, which Dougy will stutter while his dad turns into an absurdity, before uttering his automatic *no*. But he is pacified by the TV, or made indifferent. Dougy can't tell which. Optimism clouding his judgment, thinking maybe he'll ask during one of the fifteen-minute dentist commercials. He needs a few dollars to finish his plane, a few dollars for a battery, just one spark and he'll have it, thrust. But he's thinking he should leave. There's no point in even asking. But the TV goes blank, distracting him, the words *emergency broadcast system* appear, a male voice says, *Please, do not adjust your set.* Doug stares at the screen, finally something interesting, which somehow seems to make sense of the wrestling and the empire of teeth and his dad, who turns to look at him and says, *Seeing as you've got nothing to do, why don't you polish my shoes?* Infuriated with himself for letting himself get trapped, he spreads yesterday's paper on the basement floor and opens a tin of Nugget, inhaling the fumes and getting a black spot on his nose, and learning an *'at a boy* of cheap respect.

When the leg cast comes off Joanne offers to drive him to the cemetery. It's strange to have the topic in the open, the topic of his mother, exposing her, peeling back a corner of himself, to reveal this private constant. Even from the greatest distance she acts on him, gives his life what motion it has. The same currents operate with the old man, loyal to this ultimate defeat, the both of them, their cold comet tails growing the closer to her they travel. When Joanne tells him who else is coming, Doug declines. *Funny,* she says, *he backed out too,* and it shows in her face who she thinks should make the first move.

When the president being assassinated was announced over the PA, as Dougy was in the cloakroom putting on his coat to go home for lunch, the teacher

46

cried out in pain. What an amazing word: assassinated. Running home with it, hoping Mum didn't know, wanting to be the bearer of the news so he could receive her amazement. When he tried to understand the event, the best anyone could come up with was *For no particular reason.* It became a justifiable position to take on any subject, and permanently fixed the wrestlers in reality.

He limps to the store and stares at the brands of whisky. He doesn't want to drink but he needs to feel something and their labels conjure old conversations with himself. A Nugget display attracts him and he holds a tin to his cheek. In the common room he spreads a newspaper and then goes to extended care to get the shoes, taking a wheelchair because his leg is killing him. He gets on the floor and spreads the oddly viscous polish over Heckle and Jeckle. Back black, he brings up their shine, and feels strangely calm.

Cactus and Stone sits in the front as they drive out of town. Doug slumps in the back and watches Joanne and her consistently dispassionate expression, wondering what in the world motivates her. Could Christ really supplant the human lust for degradation? They drive over a rise from where the horizon is pushed back and its range revealed, like a naked body's bushy contours, its rolling grasses and fields shaved for surgery, coulees and concrete sky, with grain elevators that don't get closer no matter how long you drive at them.

And Joanne drives too fast, though Doug can see she

isn't aware of its dangers, or its pleasures. Flying over loose gravel, not nursing it but reacting to the drift, she blows by windbreaks and floors giant farm insects. Dropping down to the Saskatchewan River they cross a long narrow bridge and, catapulting up the other side, drift over the inexact centre of the road as they approach the crest. Doug stops breathing and can see the old man having the same thought: Saskatchewan roulette. Joanne asks Doug if he ever thought of accepting Christ as his savior. He's embarrassed she would ask him such a thing in front of his dad. They sail over the top with a heady sensation of reprieve when they meet nothing coming the other way.

The edge of the northern forest gradually clusters in around them as they proceed out of the parklands, leaving the aspen groves for the more profuse pine and poplar and birch prophesying boreal vastness, the shadow his mother casts a thousand miles into his heart. The smell of it is familiar, a scent he remembers but can't precisely recall, reminiscent of his grandmother's chest, the fragrance of her house.

Cactus and Stone has a voice. He and Joanne talk about the hospital and agree with each others' contradictions, while Doug listens attentively, not ready to offer thoughts of his own, feeling a familiar folding in. After they cross a wooden bridge over the Touch, Cactus and Stone says, *Turn here*, and down a narrower, dustier road they drive, turning right again after a mile and pulling up beside a whitewashed arch. Markers and crosses huddle together in the spindly trees, shy with company. There are flying squirrels here; or was that an older-cousin myth? Memories and inventions become indistinguishable in time, like the innocent levitation he experienced as a boy, which he tried to control and lost forever, finally chalked up to dreaming.

They had two services for her, the first with a gleaming casket trimmed in gold and on its way to the oven, which you couldn't help obsessing over—were they really going to burn the casket or was this just part of the overall scam of losing her, the scam of biology, of mood that comes over him like thunder, claustrophobic and ridiculous with expectation? He doesn't want to think about it. He just wants to see her headstone, to see the carved letters rustle with their warmth. He remembers leaning over impeccable red dirt, so easily scooped out, to receive the post office parcel she was in. What haunts him is the ashes, that they weren't poured naked into the earth, but sealed forever in mediocre memory. The old man stands there staring at the ground beside her, swept up in his own system of weathers, around him other members of her family: the cold fish, her grandparents, a brother . . .

They retrace the square of the farm. Driving south over the rivers, it seems so small, a parcel you can enclose without looking back. Dougy found his grandfather's World War I helmet in the barn on a nail next to grandmother's ensign. Till the end of her life she held the land in the event of World War III, when the family would be together again. It would be like Vimy, the years after, when you heard its stature in every voice. In '36 they sailed to France, the silent veterans and their eager wives, to unveil the memorial and parade through cheering crowds to banquets given in their honour attended by kings. She holds onto the land still, though her grip is less terrible, waiting for the family to join her; and they do, one at a time, obediently gather.

Driving into the steepening dusk, Doug watches the old man until he's sure he's asleep and then says to Joanne, *I am a Christian. You asked, earlier?* She looks at him; satisfied, acknowledging his melancholy smile, turning the headlights on. He really isn't, but all human fortresses are wallpaper; and if everything is a lie, the truth has got to be masquerading there somewhere.

IV   ALIEN ABDUCTIONS

DOUGY TREADS OVER the pre-dawn snow three blocks down and one block over to the pick-up box. With a dull bread knife he cuts the string binding his two bundles of Sunday Edition and loads his bag. The strap of the world digs into his shoulder, heavy with the sins of a solitary child, aching from the tips of his fingers to his jaw. He rolls papers into boxes; folded, they go through walls. Lobbing them onto porches they flutter, foreshadowing storm. He works his way down Sixth Street and then comes back up Fifth. He locates all the nameless cul-de-sacs, though this is never a given and outsmarts most of the vanishing houses.

The smell of church is fascinating. It has distinct layers if you peel it apart, pews and men's suits, floor wax, Lifebuoy soap, Bible paper. The minister makes as much sense as a barking dog. Dougy imagines himself being spoken of in the portentous rumbling, waiting with his brothers and the other children to descend to the kindergarten. Mum sits a few rows back, blissfully staring at her sons, thinking on them, remembering before they were born how she used to stroll with her girlfriends down Granville Street. In those days hit-and-run photographers caught you off guard, not framed up small and ordered to show your teeth, they took good pictures, in the days before puppy love bought you for a cheap setting. The men thought they were so sharp in their fedoras and confident of their dreams, their second war won. He used to be so attentive and intense. What she wouldn't sell for more of that, if she had something. She likes the smell of church, the furniture polish and ironing starch, toothpaste and baths. She wishes she understood the minister. Her son staring back is beautiful. The minister talks about her, how pretty she is, how intelligent.

Deep snow brings cougars out of the mountains. Pets go missing and deer take less brazen excursions into the maw of man. It's eerie to find their tracks in the light of day, telling you more about the world than you wanted to know; that the mountains don't sleep. He goes into the claw-black wind and it gives him courage to test his thumb on the serrated knife. It's impossible to be quiet on the crunchy snow, and mailboxes ring and porches thump. Only the deaf and the sleeping wouldn't know he's out there, with every cougar in the valley listening. He sees a tail above a crown of road, and a distant cry could be any number of sorry predators.

A small gray man is standing in the boys' room. They stare at him and listen to the thoughts he plants: silence is the shadow of sanity; serpents swim in shallow sleep. Something brushes Dougy's face and a point of light moves deliberately in his peripheral vision, his body paralyzed. Then it's morning and Mum is shaking him to get up to do his route.

Coming upon deer is a rare enough event. You see them standing beside arbors and under trellises and it means you're having a good day. When you find one torn to pieces, only remains, surrounded by the prints of not a cougar but dogs, what then? House pets travel in packs on the predawn streets. His breath mists and his sweating head itches. What does it take to turn Fluffy into a butcher? Does she think about violence when your back is turned, have guilty fantasies? When they get together, three or more animals, does violence become necessary? He picks up a piece of exploded animal, part of its leg. This is proof that life is too absurd to be real. He'll show it to his brothers. As though in response to his thoughts, the distance gets crowded with dogs. The body part won't drop out of his electrified grip but he is able to run. He hears the pack closing on him and he falls and his papers burst like feathers while the hounds hurtle a street over and away.

At Gyro Park lookout on a summer night they stare at the spilled-sugar sky. A star dislodges and Mum touches it with her finger. They blink and lose it and find it and hold it, because it's all they've got, this fire-fly, this gizmo where once there was God. Dougy stands on the stone wall, to get a closer look and Mum holds his ankle. One night orange and blue beams flash back and forth between the mountains. Radiant with fear, life is everything it promised.

He climbs above the town and out of city limits to the reservoir and into the red yellow forest. The trail is steep and it leads to the east away from the lake and the rising traffic sounds until there's nothing but the polite applause of the forest and the warm sun of afternoon. He wants to find the source of the beams of light, but the trail has it's own intelligence. It leads him to a sus-pension footbridge, with a perfect icing of blue leaves covering its rotting planks. He makes his way over the liquid tension and discovers it slippery with snails. A hundred feet below, silver blood soaks through the un-derbrush. The trail is unrecognizable going back and the woods get crowded with his imagination. Hermits inhabit abandoned mines. Articles of clothing turn up in odd places. The world is full of illogical business. It must be frightening to be an adult, to covet insanity and extraordinary compromise. Though children will swarm too and kill other children. Nobody knows why.

He comes out at the wrong place on the tracks, a mile north of where he expected, with a long trestle in his path. By late afternoon he's jittery with fatigue and crossing it he listens to the mountain, to every rattle in the trees, every bird's throat and boulder out for a run. Thankfully trains warn from miles away, their blast so loud you can pick it up in your hands. Walking on the ties is a jerky affair, an unpredictable mind game, being spaced too close for taking one at a time and too distant for two. He couldn't run if his life depended on it.

And then an engine materializes, sudden and appalling. Outraged, he faints, and comes to with the train over top of him, hissing and clapping like an insect, smelling of electricity and oil and coming to a full stop. The fat trestle timbers clench to the bone under the passive weight. He can hear the engineer and conductor shouting from either end, working towards him on the naked side planks. Beside him is a stage and a drum of rainwater and a ladder straight down. Slivers know the way to the bottom where a creek bed is all there is to follow home.

Mum applies iodine to his scrapes. *Did you find anything?* She asks. And he tells her about the bridge and the carpet of blue leaves, how his footprints went to the middle and stopped. He says, *I think I have a fever, feel my head*, and she does with her hand and he says, *With your lips* and so she does and says he's fine. He sleeps for a while but wakes when the gray man touches him. Believing he's unconscious they cut him open and put needles in his brain. At six Mum comes to get him up to do his route. He stands trembling in the yard, watching his breath.

V   COLLECTING SHADOWS

DOUG IS THUMBING through a box of old records while he spins the velvet platter of a record player from the fifties. Perry Como, TV Bloopers, Doris Day, and interestingly, Stravinsky's *Pulcinella Suite*. He starts the machine and puts the record on. He dips the heavy needle into the track and turns up the volume. It lifts him, and his mind expands beyond bone and dandruff.

He buys the machine and carries it home by the sturdy handle, clamping the record under his arm. The weight of it amplifies his limp; and he's soon overheated in the heavy winter coat he resurrected from the hospital storage room. He tires easily and sweats profusely. He stops to rest his poorly re-assembled frame, standing the machine on end for a place to sit.

When he listens to *Pulcinella* again he's captured by its complexity and buffoonery, the audacity of nature. When it finishes he plays it again and turns up the volume so he can hear it from the porch. The sky is heavy with winter and overdue. Across the tracks the field that was wheat is now an open wound. Beside the road, patches of grass whisper a prayer for snow.

After dark the rain begins and chatters away on the roof in a language he thinks he could have understood if he'd been born a little smarter or a little happier. In the morning the thermometer reads thirty below and last night's rain, caught before it could run away, is a thick glaze on everything. The barbs on fences are knots of glass. Spindly, leafless branches are black with varnish and more loosely drawn. He imagines porcelain children and bone china cows. The most beautiful detail is the quiet. No cars or barking dogs. Even the wind is tongue-tied, stuck to a frozen pipe somewhere.

Though he's wearing everything he owns, cold finds ways in, scurrying anxiously around under the layers next to his skin. His toes are numb and his face wears raw. Dangerous weather makes him euphoric. Outside the hospital he knocks the sand and ice from his boots. He can hear the cheap strains of electric organ through the wall. He goes in and hears the voices and recognizes the hymn. Sunday service in the common room. Outside the window, boxcars stand on a siding. On the wall is a picture of God. He listens to the voices, to a strong male dominating the withery others. Telepathy between them makes his dad self-conscious.

He lights a cigarette and pours a whisky, staring at the electric heater, the smoke rising in its waves. There is enough food and drink for the day, enough tobacco,

Pulcinella Suite. Frost patterned windows confess light and the drink purifies his thoughts. Self-hatred becomes irony and confusion mystery. The glass he drinks from was a gift from a woman. It's small and heavy, perfect for neat whiskys. He doesn't remember why he left her. He listens to the space heater's intermittent crickets. He stands outside and the fallen snow looks like a sheet on a corpse.

He always hears new things in the familiar music. It braids with his thoughts as he plays it over and over. He rolls a cigarette and sets it aside, half finished, to write something in his notepad. But the pen confines his attention. He thinks about the woman whose gift it was. He rolls it in his fingers and shines it on his shirt.

The jarring snowplow clears the tracks, piling the snow into banks. It wakes him, rescues him from a dream. It's left him empty and bored. He dresses and goes out. The snow has a thick crust, which almost holds his weight but collapses at the last second, galling him, each step a broken promise. He climbs over the bank into the icy channel. He kneels down and puts his damp mitt on the rail, and it sticks startlingly fast. He kneels close to the rail and spits to watch it freeze. Putting his tongue between his lips he leans closer, his heart beats harder making his body rock with the narcotic of stupidity. The tip of his tongue sticks. He struggles and more of it gets stuck. He feels a vibration that soon is an intimate thing, and he whimpers and gasps and his lips stick. When the engine appears in his peripheral vision he leaves a layer of his mouth on the rail. The train storms past and Doug lies panting on the no-angel snow.

He sits above the heater in its rising curtain of warm. His mouth is in agony with every drag of smoke and every hit of whisky. And *Pulcinella* has never sounded so logical and fresh. He thinks about his relationships with women. On the table he gathers their trinkets, the shot glass, the gold pen, an American silver dollar, a stone elephant, a bell. When he holds them up to the light, they cast their tiny shadows into his life. He collects shadows.

The heater stops clicking and the room begins to cool. He searches for a breaker box and finds beside the kitchen door fuses, not breakers, all with their cherry in tact. He fiddles with the space heater, bangs it with a fist, finesses the connections. He dismantles it but there isn't enough he understands. He puts his coat on and turns the oven to three hundred. Soon it's warm again.

Going for a piss he discovers the bathroom mossy with frost. The single source of heat can't deal with the cold snap. He discovers a spider in the tub and is fascinated by the creature's predicament, the unclimbable walls. Searching all the window ledges for the flies of summer he wonders what finally kills them, starvation or brain damage. He throws them in the tub but the spider isn't interested. Filling a pan with water, Doug puts it on the stove and turns on the burner. He drops in the last three wieners, but the water doesn't boil and the room starts cooling off again. This time he has blown a fuse and can find no replacements. As drunk as he can make himself he goes outside and lies in the burning snow. The sky is a road and there's been a collision. He feels cold radiate into his core and he lifts his arms to embrace the sky, but floating before him is an image of Joanne. Around her neck hangs a small silver cross. He holds her there by its delicate chain.

A sheet of plywood covers the fireplace. He removes it and pulls on the flue handle and can't remember why they told him not to use it. He brings an armload of firewood in and soon has a blaze lapping the walls with light. He lies on the floor and relaxes, tries to meditate, but he feels a tickle in his throat and he sits up into thick choking smoke. He separates the logs in the grate with his bare hands and breaks a window heaving them outside.

Disgusted with himself he lays on the floor, hopeless and tired, thinking it can't get any worse, and then sees a flame dancing in a crack in the wall. Before he can indulge in disbelief the ceiling is on fire. He slithers ahead of the flashover to the kitchen, thinking of saving his things, but *Pulcinella* is melting and his hair is on fire. He pulls a blanket over his head and crawls out the door as the house goes up like a match head.

As it grows, he moves back with the line of melted snow and instant mud, the narrow zone between freezing and cooking. It's an exhausting night, watching it burn down. By dawn he's standing beside a pile of foul embers. Wrapped in the dirty blanket, his hair singed, he walks into town.

He is able to move into one of the unfurnished independent suites attached to the hospital. He had a choice between a recently vacant one and another that's been standing empty for months. He took the one whose smells were human rather than the pervading mildew of the other. He lives on the floor and spends his time staring out the sliding window. A bag of wind rolls and gyres outside. It flattens to the road like paint and then leaps up with small furies and so progresses down the street. He has an interesting perspective of fences and clotheslines and a Chevrolet on blocks sits in one of the yards. Joanne delivers a message from his father, an invitation to come for coffee. The summons makes him jumpy. To obey is to have hope, one kind word would feed him for a month, an affectionate squeeze on the shoulder would keep him going for the lifespan of a dog. In the common room Doug hangs his coat and stands by the window. His dad is made dainty by Parkinson's and his shoes need a polish, which Doug thinks is probably why he's here. He gestures with a resigned wave at the chair he wants Doug in and takes the one opposite, hastily pausing. Having only tenuous control of his body, the signals from his brain get mixed up. He's not simultaneous, the different parts of him at different stages of doing.

So, Doug, he says, *what's your sign?*

Doug is confused by the question: *My sign? What do you mean? Aquarius? Do you mean that one?*

Aquarius? Really? That explains a few things.

What does it explain?

Oh, just . . . nothing. You were always so. . .

There is another lost moment. The old man used to get upset at the mention of anything the slightest bit flaky, like tubeless tires and greaseless bearings. Now he's talking about astrology? And what does he mean "*You were always so . . .*" what?

He has photographs he tosses to Doug across the table. Pictures of headstones, different models.

I put a down payment on that one, he says, clumsily separating out one of modest red marble. *What do you think?*

It's . . . nice, says Doug.

It's as close to your mother's as I could get. It's two thousand. I put a down payment of the three hundred I got for the Olds. There's a death benefit from the province. It's two thousand dollars. It'll come to you. All you need to do is pay the balance, seventeen hundred dollars, when you receive the benefit. With the remaining three you want to have your mother's stone restored.

Doug collects his mail at the post office. He cashes his welfare cheque. Cold rattles over the landscape, clenching shutters and cracking rivers while mice eat newspapers from chinks in the walls. Doug goes into the Lutheran church and sits there alone. The slightest human sound and he'll vanish.

His dad and the blind farmer play cards every day. His dad deals and reads both their hands. Herman follows him with some kind of radar, knowing most of what's in front of him. Doug sits nearby and watches.

There I stood, Doug's dad says, *while all my friends were off to Europe. You have a pair of fours and a pair of eight's, a one-eyed jack.*

Herman taps the table top with his wedding ring meaning that he'll keep them.

I saw the Navy, the Army, and the Air Force, he continues. *Same thing at all three. They found out I was half deaf.* He deals the cards again, reads his, then bends Herman's around to have a look. *An eight of hearts, six of spades, jack of hearts, queen of diamonds, and two tens, of clubs and spades.*

Joanne brings Doug a cup of coffee, and says to his dad, *Isn't it nice your son is here to see you again?*

Your son is here? Asks Herman.

Have you met my son? Doug, come over here.

The blind man puts out his hand, nicotine stained, cracked fingernails.

His generation doesn't understand, Doug's dad says.

Sit down, Doug, Herman says.

Doug takes a chair and crosses his arms.

Herman puts the deck down in front of him. He shuffles and deals out five cards each.

Deuces and one-eyed jacks wild, he says.

His dad gives Herman an experienced look and

Herman taps the table. His milky eyes are like sighted eyes in how they attempt to hold you, though Doug need only move his head slightly to see no corresponding movement. He wants to ask him if any light gets in; he wants to ask him if it matters.

Cactus and Stone has begun to deteriorate rapidly. His commode has a view of the parking lot. The TV is never on and his candy sits in a drawer. Herman and Doug keep up the card game and get Joanne to join in. They use braille cards Doug found through a magazine ad and since Herman is still at a disadvantage not knowing braille, they blindfold themselves and all struggle with it. Others join them and others watch. Moments of intense concentration are punctuated by gales of laughter. Somebody usually makes tea and puts out a plate of cookies. *Braille cookies*, Herman says, and they all laugh.

Doug, Herman and Joanne go for long drives in search of drive-in restaurants and points of interest, which Doug describes to Herman in purposeful prose. They visit Herman's farm, which doesn't belong to him now and isn't a farm anymore for that matter, its fields assimilated by neighbours, the buildings cut off at the knees and transported elsewhere. The barn is all that remains. Surrounded by spindly young birches, its roof beam sags and the west wall is in collapse, wildness weaving the structure into its own designs. Blank-eyed creatures inhabit it now without irony. They understand copper tubes and galvanized troughs in their own way. Through gaps in the shrinking lumber small birds shuttle their cargo of blades of grass.

Doug visits Cactus and Stone, who asks him:

How are you? How are you settling in?

Oh, fine, says Doug.

That's nice. I'm glad you came to see me.

It's nice to be here.

I enjoyed your service last Sunday.

I'm glad.

In very little time everything habitual in the face is unmade. It has all the symmetry of a pile of rags though the anger is still present, at least its afterglow. He could turn it on and off like a stove. With it he could smoke you out or sell you anything.

Has he retreated in terror or plunged forward courageously? Doug doesn't know. There is only this slug that gives no clues, this elaborately extended definition, with its wires and tubes and battery of technicians. Lying there all-important, grotesque and impotent, Doug is not afraid of him now. The room of solitude he built around himself had rooms within rooms that required lodgers: your freedom, your vitality. Doug feels something though it isn't love, sentiment maybe, the stunted little survivor. He stands over the sooty eyes but they stare at a vague spot beside him.

At news of the death, delivered by an attentive Joanne,

he sits by the window and watches the snow sag untidily. Later he plays cards with Herman and is glad the man can't see his flushed and healthy face. Twenty years younger he looks. He's just grateful the proper distance has been restored.

Doug's brothers and sister come in from Edmonton, Toronto, Prince George. The four of them stand on the sidewalk in front of the funeral parlour with an aunt and uncle from Kelowna. The spring air is nervous with chill. They appear nothing alike but their mannerisms mesh: the diffident regard, the restless hands. Even given their estrangement, the sibling closeness is palpable and exclusive.

Doug is holding the box. This is the smallest room yet, and heavier than he imagined it should be, as though some of the flesh and blood remains, and it makes him queasy. They consider it thoughtfully, nodding earnestly like disappointing children. Auntie says, *Don't open it; he'll be all over town before you know it.*

The box rides in the front for a while until Doug gets antsy and hands it over the seat to Don who puts it on the floor. After a few more miles they pull over and put him in the trunk, turn him into cargo; it's all they can do.

Doug places him on the roof for a last look around. Other cars pull in, cousins, eight of them. Doug doesn't remember these people though they seem to know him. Herman and Joanne and a few others from the hospital arrive. Olaf, one of the cousins, has a posthole digger and with it easily removes enough earth for the box. The minister arrives in his station wagon and performs an atheist's rights, bread and butter for the ministry, followed by a greatest hit, The Lord's Prayer. He places the box into the hole with some final gibberish and formality is abandoned for practical concerns. Someone produces a piece of lumber and holds it upright in the hole while Olaf replaces the earth. Don writes the name in black felt marker.

At Olaf's farm they have bitter coffee with butter-thick cream. The sandwiches are disconcertingly bland. Doug gets coffee for Herman and Joanne when they arrive. Olaf leads a tour of the farm. It's a collection of pieces added to pieces, nothing is harmonized. Patch jobs go unpainted, additions remain the colour of past lives, and new shingles stand out like scar tissue. Chickens live in a lean-to of corrugated fibreglass, and the goats occupy an old house trailer with a ten-year-old Ontario license plate. Joanne takes Doug aside. She wants to give him something. It's a small cross. And he doesn't know what to say, which she finds eloquent.

Back inside, the conversation turns to the service, and someone asks Doug about the headstone. He tells them that it's ordered, that it's red marble. *As close to Mum's as possible,* he says, and what the inscription will say: *Beloved Husband of . . .* His dad's words, a cliché. His dad never liked people as far as Doug could tell.

But here they are at the end of his life, a roomful. Can that be it, after you've sluiced all the rest away, the heavier ore?

He sits across a wide oak desk from a man in a grey suit. There's a family connection between them Doug didn't quite catch. They're going over specifications for the stone, checking the spelling. Joanne and Herman are waiting in the car. They're on their way to Prince Albert where another cousin has invited them for dinner. The undertaker gives his pen to Doug so he can sign the contract, and then removes himself, used to people needing time alone with their signatures. Doug counts the hundred dollar bills onto the desk, twenty of them. The price of immortality, cheap really, when you think about it. He puts the money back in his wallet and leaves.

He's quiet for the hour drive to Prince Albert, brooding heavily. He gets Joanne to stop at the airport where the lone agent confirms a flight south due in an hour, which Doug pays for from his sheath of hundreds. Leaning over the car he springs it on them. Joanne stares like she's been shot and Herman lets out an insulted groan. Doug isn't willing to talk about it. No, coming here in the first place was a mistake. From inside the building he watches the car pull reluctantly away. It stops at the end of the parking lot and Joanne stands up out of the car in a flash of reflected light. From out of the north a four-prop DC something comes

in and Doug is the only one boarding. Rattling air-
borne, tongues whisper around him. He listens to their
cadence and caress. Without meaning, it's music. He
looks at Joanne's gift. What just happened? Below
them is sliced earth and hazy sky. The wilderness is not
out there.

THRILL KILL

S MALL VOICES WARN YOU AWAY from the on-
rushing path of sudden mortal danger, or carry
you over bizarre detours to a lost friend who says she
was just thinking about you; weightless as a flake of an-
gel dandruff landing on your shoulder, riveting as a
child's call from a mile away, though when you turn
you can comprehend nothing but a fading memory of a
fading echo. George wasn't listening when an inkling
told him the oil light was broken, that he should get it
checked, and an hour later the engine seized up nearly
costing him his job. Or the time one hot Friday night he
picked up a seedy couple out of context in the British
Properties because he reasoned his anxiety about them
was just paranoia. Code 100 was for emergencies,
though you imagined it played down, in contained cri-
sis, falteringly but with poise, not wailed on like
George that night, between outraged sobs that he'd
been robbed and assaulted. My fare was a little dismayed,
as was I, though George's presence of mind to follow his

assailants speeding off in another car improved our opinion. In minutes the police commandeered the air and George was relaying his position to them via Jack Merryweather, our dispatcher.

Shut down, the other drivers pulled alongside one another and sat their noses in the radio, nodding to each other, ambivalence towards George congealing into at least deference, if not respect. He stayed with them through uncooperative streets, tailing their dog-tracking Merc to a parking garage in Burnaby where the police closed in. The episode lasted for over half an hour during a busy time of day; and when we counted up our tips and handed in our sheets we could see how much money it had cost us.

George married an unpleasant woman named Margaret, who took charge of his life and put him through some basic training in the husbandly arts, the grounding of her lightning, and walking on eggshells. The more extraordinary she tried to make the wedding the more mundane it had to be. It was a wedding. The usual expressions of commitment rang as hollow as they generally did. It was somebody's dream-to-end-all-dreams, pathetic to everyone but she and her diffident groom. Merryweather and I were the only guests from among the people George worked with. I went because I didn't know how to say no, and Merryweather? Who knows. Glum and antsy, even with his gorgeous wife all medium-rare beside him, he couldn't stop making snide comments about the bride.

The ceremony naturally didn't have the results Margaret expected. The sacredness she had wanted to bleed from it to the rest of her life was just aspirin magic. Her expectations collapsed on the lawn under the sheer weight of the light of day. Trying to keep her courage up, she went through the A to Z of anti-depressants, each one providing the placebo of optimism, but for no more than a few days.

Margaret was good for George though. She goaded him into giving up driving and pointed him in the direction of the car rental industry where he was hired and measured for a maroon jacket. His wick burned brightly behind the big counter as he guided people through the forms and scanned their cards, rarely soiling his hands with cash. It was getting so you viewed a person with a cash deposit as lacking morally somehow.

He brought home flowers and watched them bend, turning their vase once in a while to watch them bend from a different angle. Life wasn't exactly happy but it was better than suicide, he thought, and Margaret's moods were a reliable distraction from his own flatness. And what could he do, he'd married the woman? He would just have to learn the complicated hydraulics of her needs and keep steering into the wind during her attacks of despair, which were, when he thought about it, displays of her potential to love him. With teasing and indulgence he'd nurse her back from depression to indifference, and for him it was enough.

He was in the car rental business for three months when he was laid off. Neither of them had any savings and when he was turned down for UIC benefits there was only driving taxi. A voice in his head told him not to, but his wallet said he had no choice.

Back with Precision he stayed close to Zone One, taking seniors to restaurants and malls, a comfortable pace for him. As much as possible he stayed out of competition for airport runs and away from downtown. Every afternoon at five-o-five he crossed the bridge to pick up the eighty-year-old Mrs. Stinson at the track. He enjoyed driving onto the site behind the fences and around the cones where cars were not normally allowed, shifting through the hypnotized crowds and around stalled livestock. He pulled up a little early so he could enjoy the smells and sights of interesting work. Even the horses led better lives than his. We can't all be kings, he thought. And a good thing, he supposed. It was bad enough the way it was, living in a skin woven from his fears.

The old woman, shrunk to the size of absolute necessity, folded herself like a lawn chair into the back seat, while George held an umbrella over her. She gave him the address and explained in detail how to get there, which made him smile patiently. Each day it was the same; she greeted him like a stranger and gave him the same instructions. For weeks this went on and it sucked the vitality from his calm and he began to feel invisible and unspecified. His attempts to avoid her by getting out of Zone One failed. Her call always came through five minutes after his shift started and he couldn't drive that fast or take shortcuts enough to get over the boundary to another. One day, he edged in with, *Yes ma'am, I know the way.* Back at the office Merryweather told him she had complained and was taking her business elsewhere. He told George to watch his P's and Q's and repeated his zone one bread and butter speech. *Look, these old folks may be irritating as hell, but . . .*

He pulled up beside the poetry of debt. *Prices slashed. Two full years to pay!* A shadow divided from the shadows and climbed in. He had given up trying to engage his passengers. It was too forced, and who really listened? He didn't know enough about anything to be interesting, and if he tried, he came across as eccentric, or half-mad. When traffic on the causeway halted he glanced in the mirror to remind himself she was there. *Must be an accident on the bridge*, he said, but thought it more likely a jumper tangled in the coaxing. What's the attraction in that approach, he wondered, to complicate your last seconds with such exploding terror? But maybe it's a peaceful thing, the lost grip, the fall into arms of such certainty.

My sister was killed by a taxi, his passenger suddenly

said. *She was walking across the street and he ran her down. It was a Precision, like you.*

George looked back at her, *Oh, really?* He was trying to sound sympathetic and at the same time not gullible.

It might have been this car, she said. *What's its number?*

He told her and she relaxed a little.

No, it wasn't this one, it was 45. You ever drive it?

He assured her that he hadn't.

I've ridden it, wanted to, she said.

Moving slowly across the bridge, he went over his earthquake prayer in his head. Pulling up in front of her building the woman came around to his window.

What do you think of my sister being killed by you? she asked, in her complicated voice.

It's terrible, he said, feeling used. When she started to dig through her purse for coins to tip him he got the feeling she'd throw herself under his wheels just to get one over on him. He refused the sweating change she held out and drove away.

Back at the office, Merryweather was waiting for him. The woman had complained and George was forced to explain himself. He said he hated to be laughed at and Merryweather said, *Pride can't stop a bullet.* George found he didn't believe it himself.

If experienced drivers weren't scarce as hen's teeth . . . Merryweather threatened.

George fumed and thought it was time to look for a new job. But the next day he wasn't angry and it was easier just to report for his shift. When he looked at his wife, he didn't feel the nausea that had come to characterize his feelings and he could just make out a silhouette of how much they had felt, once, when they were planning the wedding, both surprised by their passion. Margaret packed his lunch and gave him an optimistic shove out the door. Why should he doubt his decision to marry her? She was his best friend. He had dredged his heart to make a channel for her. Words didn't appear when he needed them and he choked on ideas like fish bones, but with Margaret he could express himself and he grasped what it meant to have somebody listen.

In a parking lot over the harbour he muttered the lunch code to his hand and sat back to enjoy the night air and the outlines of ships in English Bay, turning the prickly volume on Merryweather down. Margaret's well-meaning lunch turned out to be a poorly made baloney sandwich with too much butter and only one slice of meat, no lettuce. She wasn't very good at sandwiches. And she didn't want children. There seemed little point to the marriage. After a few pulpy bites he relaxed and wondered why he had to hate what he loved.

Two men approached and asked if he was available. He didn't like the look of them and said he was on lunch. As they walked away in search of another cab he called them back, to recapture his good mood by being generous. Putting his lunch under the seat he wiped the crumbs off his shirt. He didn't like their carbon copy faces, young guys in suits, but they were just assholes and George was an asshole magnet. They crossed the second narrows bridge. One of them asked how long he'd been a cab driver. He thought about it. *At least ten years between other jobs and periods off,* he said. They asked if he'd run into much trouble. *No, not really. We don't carry much cash, and robberies are way down.* They drove south on Boundary and then east on Marine. It was going to be a profitable trip. South again down a long thin road to a park beside the river. He pulled up where they told him and one handed a fifty over the seat, said keep the change. He felt the hairs on his neck tingle. Then he was conscious of the bill, smooth sticky with his blood and he realized he had been dead for a long time. The police called it a thrill kill. A new expression was born, and George was finally one of us.

For the funeral, the streets around St. Andrews Wesley were lined with taxis, black ribbons on their antenna, polished and united. The qualities George possessed in life were finally being noticed and enlarged: he was a patient man, a kind man. When the solemn cabbies expressed their sorrow to Margaret, the deepest part of it was fear for themselves. Jack Merryweather felt duty-bound to contribute; his being on dispatch the night of the killing added poignancy to the eulogy. Though it was filled with half-truths and clichés, he rose to the occasion and delivered it with passion. He called it ritualistic, the murder of a Vancouver cabby every few years. He called it a dangerous profession and said it elevated men to the status of soldiers.

Nobody knew what he meant by that, least of all the women, but they liked it and lined up to shake his hand and make donations to the grieving widow fund he had set up on Margaret's behalf.

This was what Merryweather had needed: to stand before his comrades and feel strong. He'd been losing his grip privately for years and these past few months since his wife walked out had been witness to a terrifying slide. He was pilfering money from the company and he drank every night until he passed out. And when despair slipped past the chemicals, he cut himself with utility blades, creating new black scrawls beside the white ones from lows past. As he delivered his sermon he grasped the lectern like a steering wheel. His voice resonated in the cavities of everyone's broken dreams. Even Margaret had to hand it to him, how well it went. And she noticed his modesty bloom. It had taken him two bottles of wine to compose. Deep into his soul he cut to find the words and was intrigued to discover them there. It was one of his finest hangovers.

But the next day he felt like dirt again and had a desire to sink as low it was possible for a man to sink, to have one foot in the grave and the other in filth. When he had finished the service something snapped and he knew the further he fell the higher his exaltation would soar, and knowledge of this knowledge excited him further, sealing his fate, and down he went. He clawed impotently at the walls for a few weeks, but it was no good, and soon he found himself touching down in Rio de Janeiro; on him, every penny of the widows' fund.

He wanted to be devoured by the desperate city and got himself a small, cheap room and paid outrageous prices for hookers of every ilk. He tried new combinations of drugs and self-abuse and sometimes came close to satisfaction. But in the ashes of his purges he always found the spark of lust and understood finally that he would die. But to postpone it was the trick, to tease it. Thinking about murder gave him hours of joy. He dabbled in plans and window-shopped for ways. He needed to intensify it a little each day to get the same hit, until he had no choice but to choose a victim. Heart pounding he bought a switchblade and tested the theory on himself that edge isn't really there. The width of a molecule, visible only by proxy, by skin. He stalked a girl until she turned on him, and the game played out. Killing was for greater hearts than his.

He went to drown himself in the sea, tossing his clothes aside, the engorged city prodding him on. He was a poor swimmer but felt strong and slowly swam out into the bay, to the rightful ending of hope. He chuckled, finally an end to illusion, and with renewed enthusiasm he put one arm in front of the other, hauling in fate, dreaming one last dream. Soon he'd be folded into a wave and drowned like a kitten in a barrel. But then his hands were grasping sand and he was on a fringe of shore where tears meant nothing.

A group of children stood over him until he stirred

and they ran away. He looked back at the sea. The inconstant whore. Why not me?

He flagged a taxi down. Through the chilly night the road jiggled him and he quivered with goose bumps until he was intoxicated, contented. Was this it? This? To be purged of heat. To shiver! He was finally there. But lust sparked. Peace would betray him again.

After the funeral Margaret gave George's clothes to the Salvation Army and his tools to Value Village and his 8-track tapes to a neighbour along with the machine that played them. She donated his books to the lunchroom at work and sent his driver's license and papers in a shoebox to his vegetable mother.

She marveled at how little he had. Where most people hold onto their shed skins, George kept nothing. He thought he didn't have a right to take up more space than was necessary. And for this she was grateful. It only took a few afternoons for all traces of him to vanish.

Though she tried to put in an appearance of mourning, secretly she was glad to be alone again. She had married him because he worshipped her, and it was nice to feel powerful. But when she looked at her big little man, with his irrelevant face, she couldn't help wondering.

She decided to quit her job and dreamed about starting over somewhere, recollecting that feeling of newness when you've moved and that all-too-brief period when the people you meet are open to you. It was having too much time on her hands that brought home how much she missed George. His voice echoed in hollows left by earlier losses: her parents to bitterness, her charm to adulthood, her innocence to Santa Claus. When she went to Precision to pick up her money, she discovered a new manager in Merryweather's place and no one who knew anything about the fund. It had grown with the help of local media to twelve thousand and some odd dollars. When Margaret contacted them again they ran a picture of forlorn her and a few lines. Everyone was being nice but no one could bring anything back.

She asked to be reinstated to her job but was politely refused. They used empty words like *downsizing* and *skill-set*. It was a terrible shock to her, and she began to really miss her man. She got his tapes back and spent her days listening to James Last and Brazil 66, and drinking whisky sodas. Spike Jones and the City Slickers could make her weep uncontrollably, and she stopped bathing. For hours at a time she scraped chunks of dead skin from her scalp with ragged nails.

When a letter arrived from Rio she stared uncomprehendingly at the return address. Inside were scrawled three words: *I am sorry*. Her first thought was that it was George, a letter from the grave or that he had faked his death to escape her. Then she realized it was Merryweather and she wondered how she knew that. What was she to him? She was intrigued. If his conscience were as big as his deceit he would have to be a passionate man.

She put the letter in a drawer where it stayed for a few weeks. One night she turned off the TV and tried to compose a reply. She didn't know what she wanted to say though something pressed her from inside. She had a couple of drinks and still the words didn't come. She never used to drink but now it kept her company. She finally wrote, *Are you OK?* With a couple of extra stamps for good luck she dropped it in the red box, and a month later, standing on the steps, she read the single word reply: *No.*

After a terrible flight that cost her everything, Margaret found herself in a beat-up taxi going through *National Geographic* streets. Everywhere she looked were images torn from books and collages. She closed her eyes to calm her beating ocean. Definitely this was the stupidest thing she had ever done.

At the top of a cramped staircase she knocked. Pushing the door, she saw Merryweather lying on a bare mattress. The hostage air stung her eyes. The room was an aftermath, and flies owned the place. A small gun in his hand, his gaze moved to look at her. Clearing a chair she sat down. All fear left her.

He smiled, only to express resentment, and refused to speak. She put food on the table and liquor in his cup and when he was stronger they went out for walks.

He tenderly ravaged her clunky body, her hairy legs and terrible breasts. He loved that she was unencumbered by beauty so easily lost in the corner of his eye. She was free and clear, no payments due on expectations. And she lusted too, for her skinny thief with his honest-to-god passion, his song of captivity so eloquently etched all over him.

And so the world came to them, rock and storm. The yellowed newspaper article about George's death was tacked to the wall, though something about the face was no longer vague. In light of an exploding universe he was remarkably calm, a mountain in a cage. But they had no words for what he meant to them.

When Jack was better he drove a taxi, though being away from her his fear rose like a tidal wave, and he hurried home to cling. She listened to his day and all the terrifying stories that made it up, which lapped around them and gently rocked them.

THE CAR

STAN WALKS DOWN THE HALL gawking into rooms with opened doors, his Parkinson tremors in remission giving him time to notice things. The lamentably loud television sets, and how sterile the fluorescent lights make everything seem and the million telephones, all the time chirping like cicadas. It's given him time to think in the abstract about things like integrity and personal power, in short supply around a place like this. He pulls his hearing aid out to mute the voices. Doctors visit like weather, are praised and criticized like weather. Stan's doctor comes sporadically, the urgency out of his condition with the right balance of medications. The weather has bestowed on him finally a few good months.

He unstacks chairs to create a semicircle and drags a table out to the front. Walking backwards with it is risky and he can't afford a fall. The staff would swirl around him like newspapers in a vortex, with lots of pulling and no helping and always resentment. He sits down at the table to get a feel for it, the president's chair. This was his idea, a residents' association to deal with the staff and their toothless justice. Nobody loves a dictator yet everybody wants to be one. He clasps his hands on the table and stares at the assembled furniture, not happy with the arrangement, but resigned.

He makes his way to his room and falls asleep. Two hours later he wakes up unable to move. From experience he knows to relax, brain signals work best when he's not trying. With the pole beside his bed he pulls himself up. Changing his shirt, he goes back to the common room.

The old people have begun to fill the chairs. Dropping his pad and pens on the table, he goes to fetch Mother. He parks her on the end of the front row where she twists around to see who's behind her. He watches her self-conscious hands knead a crumpled tissue while he listens to the babble spilling out behind him, flooding the room. It wouldn't take much more to drown him.

He stands up and faces them, holding the back of a chair for balance, and trying to push his once powerful voice over the gossip, he says, *Welcome to the first meeting of our new association. The first order of business is to elect a president. It seems there is only one . . . contestant, me.* He doesn't like the word, it's not correct. He uses it to hide how important this is to him. But he ends up sounding desperate. He continues, *To make this legal we should have a show of hands.*

Thirty "for" and none "opposed" with one "abstention," his mother, who is only slightly aware of the fact she's not in her room. He planned to introduce a second item of business, but already they're restless and Mother is pushing unpromisingly on her wheels. He closes the meeting and takes her to her room. On the way he notices a new ad tacked to the bulletin board, *For Sale, '79 Oldsmobile, good condition.* He's not in the market for a car.

At the next meeting he's better prepared, and he enlists the help of Mrs. Lord, whose job will be to take minutes and to keep the others in their seats. Her delicately ruined hands caress the pad of foolscap he gives her. He picks up his gavel, a croquet mallet he found in the storage room, sips from the water glass beside him and smiles at Mrs. Lord. He opens the meeting and formally introduces her, to make it official, and pushes on to his first item of business.

We need to create some kind of . . . something, for the fair and reasonable treatment of residents, he says.

On a whim he calls the owner of the Oldsmobile, who offers to drive it over for a look-see. It has power windows and power steering, a V-8 and no rust. The finish is chipped in a few places but obviously well looked after. He climbs in and his limbs obey with no clowning, no struggle.

The man says, *Take her for a long drive; she needs it. Call me at home when you get back.*

Stan is pleased to be with it. When he drops the lever into drive he feels it strain against his foot. The buildup of inertia holding him in place snaps, and he's free. Miraculously absent from the wheel is his Parkinson's shimmy. And the accelerator cradles his foot, not affected by small tremors. He turns onto the highway and, surprised by so much power, is going a hundred and climbing, his foot not obeying, though only for half a second. He cruises to the next town turning back at the water tower, just like he did as a boy running errands for his father. Stan has never owned a car of this quality. Too rich for a salesman's blood. He drove Galaxies, a Fairlane; one company leased him a Plymouth station wagon; and an Impala four-door. Back at the home he pulls into the space nearest his window and calls the owner to ask if he'll take a cheque. By suppertime he has it insured and while the light lasts he stares out the window at it. His first Olds.

When he moved to BC in his early twenties he went into selling because of the freedom it gave him. He sold tractors to farmers, skidders to loggers, giant shovels to open pit mining operations. He knew every road in BC and on weekends, if he was home, took the family for drives south over the Salmo Creston or west to Christina Lake to fish on the main lake, over Coffee Creek bluff. He drove them into strip mines dodging Euclids and up logging roads where you listened for the blast of horns and drove into the ditch or up on a bank to let the log carriers barrel past. Once a year they drove through the Rockies and, like nothing else could, the mountains restored him and connected him to his family. Turning home at dusk he taught the boys to identify makes and years of cars by their silhouette and the configuration of their lights.

After Kathy died he moved back to live in a trailer in Mother's yard. He made a fair enough living during those years, selling water purifiers and cutting keys, traveling between Prince Albert, Melfort, and Saskatoon. He got to know farmers in the area, and made regular visits to see his cousins, and drove to the cemetery every chance he got.

Stan tells the nurse he's leaving for a few days but she wants him to talk to the doctor first. He says, *I'm informing you of my intentions, not asking your advice.* He tells Mother he'll be back in a couple of weeks though in the back of his mind he has no intention of returning. Why did he wait so long? Mother doesn't need him now. He wants to see his children. He needs to see the city again. He lugs the key cutting machine out of the storeroom just in case he feels like doing some selling on the way.

Driving through Love he sees how small it is, how tiny the houses are and how dry the lawns. *Love;* funny they would call a town that, probably after someone, a John Love or some such, the first man to plant a wife here, have sons. Stan's sons haven't stayed married. They are underemployed and absentee. At highway velocity he drives towards a water tower growing slowly out of the earth, the letters of its town not yet legible. What will they spell: Joy, Faith? A cruel joke. How empty the prairies are.

Traffic is heavy in Prince Albert, where much is unfamiliar, video stores, fishbowl restaurants. He's tempted to turn off through the old town to get his bearings, but decides to stay on the highway where the gas stations are. Their patented colours stand out like desert flowers and he longs to pull in, but self-serve signs put him off and reaching the end of the strip all he's left with is a disappointing Cash-N-Save.

Fill 'er up.

You want me to check the oil?

Yes, and check the tire pressure if you don't mind . . . and the coolant, please . . . and don't forget the windows.

The attendant is reluctant and slow. People used to be glad to do things for Stan. To the office for a washroom key and around the side of the building. He stares at himself in the peeling mirror. Turning north occurs to him, maybe go as far as the cemetery. It's been a year since the time his mind slipped its crank. He drove over a group of children in a playground. A hallucination so real he needed to tell someone, and called one of the boys, but when he expressed more hurt than he meant to, the walls went up. He sold the car shortly after that.

He asks the vacant attendant if he needs any keys cut. Feeling Kathy's presence encourages him to continue west. He talks to her.

In the glove box I have an emergency candle and a flashlight and a space-age blanket. I have some cash and a MasterCard. The car is in perfect working order. Just put a bead on the horizon and fall forward. What's so hard about that?

He notices the tremors in his hand have begun again.

Now that she's gone she's all there is. *How many summers did we return to the prairies? The kids in the back seat sulking, mile after mile of still, small talk lost.* A car in a hurry flashes by, the driver craning to look at Stan, who realizes he's only doing twenty.

Ahead a restaurant comes into view under a Husky sign. Getting out of the car is difficult. His leg gets jammed in the door and he has to heave it. From the trunk he gets his sports jacket, his medications in one of the pockets. His right foot drags and the cane shakes. Keeping the tip a few inches from the ground, he's too embarrassed to actually use it. He carries it to manipulate. He orders a clubhouse and when the waitress brings him water he'll take his pills. Looking around at the travelers, the families violated by the road, the truckers hardened by it. The salesmen thrive away from their families. But that doesn't sound right. Hotel rooms smell of sanitizer, and then there's that disconcerting Bible.

The childproof tops he manages though this is never a given. He shakes a pill from each onto the table and lifts them to his mouth using the other hand as a stabilizer, only spilling a little water on his lap. His lunch in a doggy bag he makes his way to the men's room, managing to get into a stall without a hassle. The cool seat is a balm to his ragged confidence. Walls hold him in tender privacy and he feels the muscles of his face relax. Back in the car he eats the sandwich and when the medication takes effect his hand doesn't shake so much. Wiping the crumbs off his lap he pulls back onto the highway.

It keeps going through my head; I killed that old man with the Studebaker. You drove past with the kids when the police were measuring the scene. It was different after that you said, and with the business going down . . . . A car is honking because he's slowed to twenty again, and he honks back, pushing on the accelerator. It keeps happening and progress is a creep. At a rest area he manages to walk around the car a few times. He raises his arms and pushes his elbows back. He stops every hundred miles to repeat the same routine, each time with greater difficulty, each time with greater need.

He forgot how long it takes to get anywhere driving, how the minutes become hours. When he stops again for gas he has the attendant bring out bags of toffee, chocolate bars, potato chips, Canada Dry. In awhile it's all eaten and he feels worse and has to pull over and piss at the night. He pleads with it for a bed.

It's two in the morning when he reaches Lethbridge. A tv-stunned man emerges from somewhere and Stan pays for a ground floor room. He scratches the key on the doorknob and lays his jacket on the chair by the bed. He goes into the bathroom and turns on the tap, putting the stopper in. And then it strikes, the thing he fears most. He freezes up tight as wood and it's all he can do to balance there, his hands in a gesture of reaching. Water gushes into the sink, evacuated under the rim. He'd put them together for the first time in his life and pray if he could. He pisses himself and works his joints like rusted pliers, the faucet hissing and the valve choking, the mirror thankfully steamed up so he doesn't have to look at himself. He's at it for an hour before he can get the tap, and another hour to reach the bed and eat his medications and kick his clothes off. He pulls the sheet over his head. His radium watchface glows. Ancient tears don't fall but crumble.

At the Air Force induction centre in Saskatoon a doctor moves a tuning fork beside Stan's head. He writes something on a form and tells him he's sorry. The next day Stan tries the Navy. The men seem poorer but the tests are the same and the results the same. At the Army, he imagines the brassy guns of Europe and the clear snap of a twig. But it was no good. They didn't want him for the most important event of the century, and on a triviality. So he stole a car and made his first trip through the Rockies to the coast. Maybe the war was important but it doesn't match the invention of the automobile, the putting of the world on wheels. Where would Hitler be without the car? Kneeling in horseshit, cowering in Napoleon's shadow. Henry Ford is the one they'll remember.

In the morning, feeling better than he expected, he exercises, takes his medication and shaves. He opens the night table drawer to see if it's there, Gideon's Bible, and sure enough. He's never read it. It seemed like a joke whose purpose was for the amusement of cynics. He throws it on the back seat, recalling something about Christ preferring thieves.

He carries on west and in a few hours can see the Rockies driving up out of the middle distance with their blue wall that dwarfs the sky. Seeing them he realizes he can't reach them. He gets out of the car. This is what he came to remember, their feeling, how they keep his brutal heart, where hardness is prized, and he can hold his wrong ideas and not be wrong.

It doesn't matter how long it takes us. Let them honk. On the prairies you can never drive fast enough anyway. The telephone poles whip by like static on a TV screen. And once we discovered a yellow bird dead in the grill. I put a hand on one of the boys' shoulder and said, You see, that proves we were flying.

GROMAN CREEK

THE MOUNTAIN RESEMBLES a sleeping elephant, with its gaunt cheek and shattered tusk, conceding to time its memories of stone, but for the trick of balancing the sun along its silhouetted trunk, and in gathering the cirrus clouds above, so luminously orange that everything beneath seems lit from inside: behind us the rising outlook of town and the flaming red pylons of the city wharf and my daughter's shrewd and comfortable face. She watches the lake subtly moving, and the tip of the sun, making connections she doesn't think of sharing. Her shadow is long and, careful not to step on it, I indulge myself in her worship.

I haven't seen her angry or selfish and don't know her favourite colour or if she's sexually active yet. And the tragic parts of my past, which belong to her though she's unaware, are just crumpled rumours and comically mixed up in her memory with hippies and disco. We've come for our summer week, to pick up our dialogue. She knows well enough her part and lets me play out fortune's father while I can.

I want to call her Katie but she prefers Kate and my desire to respect her overrules my need to fawn and manipulate. She calls me Dad, remarkably clear of the plea and curse which usually attends that harsh word. What most fathers take in stride for me is the greatest possible pleasure, her faint and clever mockery. *Dad* . . . It's a title I've had to earn, to pay for with skin and crow, with watchfulness and irony. We talk like buddies, and she refers to *her parents* often enough, her mother and the man who's been there for years, steady as the days.

Around the bend where the lake becomes the river, skidding over the uncommitted currents, a speedboat appears. Even from this far off I know it's Ray, in the way the boat skips not directly for us but obliquely, and the way it leans, with its solitary occupant. Already I feel the old gravity, the nauseating love. He turns sharply in, as though on a whim, and knowing just when to cut the engine he makes use of the wake to carry him the last few feet. Without breaking focus to greet us, he secures the lines while a small dog jumps out to sniff our shoes. My brother and I shake hands and examine how far time has dragged us.

A cookie-cutter hotel has been built on the waterfront and a trolley line predating our history here was restored a few years ago. Heritage fronts are everywhere and updated buses pulsate through the summer streets dusty with winter sand. A little has changed in Nelson and much has not, the population roughly where it was a hundred years ago when it was famous for gold. After a decade of decline in the seventies, it backdropped a couple of movies. Something locals believe put them on the map, though Ray wonders. The Stars and Stripes flew over city hall for weeks after the shooting stopped.

He looks critically at our bags, a guitar that will likely stay in its shell, umpteen changes of clothes, and the optimism I brought more of than is useful here. I take the seat facing the stern and wet-paws keeps going for my lap. I look around for life jackets but can only hope drowning isn't painful and that the cushion Kate's sitting on floats. Perched on his seat back to see over the filmy windshield, Ray cuffs the throttle. Clearing us of the stage and a floatplane, he punches it and we plow out to bigger water. Between the three of us and our baggage the boat won't plane so he relaxes the throttle and resigns to the pace. He smiles and throws a ritual punch into my shoulder and I grin insanely, waving my fist. He asks Kate how she's doing in school and she tells him *fine*. I check out the new homes along the shore, mostly all window, jet boats under blue tarps, and stairs built into cliffs.

The first summer I brought Kate here we left after a few days. I had soaked up nostalgia like a sponge and I could barely breathe. Every building was soft with my memories of it. Every blade of grass seemed to grow importantly. Every face I studied for a childhood friend buried there and Ray was like a too accurate mirror. I told him and Carol that Kate was homesick. It's the kind of thing parents do, isn't it, children our eager scapegoats? Invert their talents and sell them back as flaws. My old man made me fearful because I was bold. But who did that to him, and how far does this dark strand trace? An impact winter remembered in our DNA, which keeps us living under rocks?

Careening into the bay, Ray maneuvers alongside a logjam decked with misfit lumber and fastened with hazards. I secure the boat to anchor rings next to a boat on the bottom, its comical slipknots still holding from last year. The unsecured plank to the shore sags under the weight of our stuff. Squeezing into the 4x4 cab with the dog, we pitch and roll up the steep loose road.

Coming onto Ray and Carol's property I look for the disillusioning spectacle of a rusted car in the pasture. But it's gone and Ray explains about the backhoe they hired to bury it, along with dead appliances that lived in the yard. Scraps of lumber litter the ground around the cabin. A heavy-duty Weed Eater lies on the porch. Two old dogs come out from under the trailer, barking and escorting us up the driveway. The twenty acres sit in the nape of Elephant's neck and is comparatively level. The government road bisects it and runs up between their neighbours into the billowing green high above, fourteen kilometres from the lake to the transmission tower on top. Their new modular came up the road, dragged all the way by a DC10 Cat and a crew of cursing men. The original cabin has been demoted to guesthouse and to where Ray's guns and rods are kept, and his recording equipment, his cassettes heaped on the bookshelf.

Bear use a path that climbs parallel with the creek up into the alpine and which Ray uses to fish the higher pools and whisper to the water. Black bears are common and last year a young grizzly came to eat apples from their tree. Ray went out with a camera while the dogs set up a row in the trailer. Worried they were going to damage something he let them out and the agile bear vanished. That encounters are rare Ray offers as reason not to be concerned.

When the dishes are in the drying rack we break out the jujubes and potato chips and a game of *Trivial Pursuit*. Questions about JFK and Abraham Lincoln seem to make every category so we invent the "Too American" rule. Invoked, it gets you another question. Katie vacillates between the "adult" questions and the "children's," settling for the latter. Complaining it makes it too easy for her, Ray tries one: *What was Grandpa Smurf's middle name?* Outside the dogs charge noisily into the forest.

Kate and I make our way to the cabin over uneven

ground, my flashlight beam dancing in front of us, both thinking about the same thing and knowing the dogs would have alerted us already doesn't make it easier. Inside it's cold and we debate for the loft, which I lose because I had it last year. Kate climbs the ladder and comments on the missing guardrail. Ray has been covering the insulation with plywood and preparing to build stairs. I find this news alarming and tell her to remember to be careful. I make sure the door is closed and the flimsy latch thrown. It's not much, but all I've got. I make up the foldout and groan with displeasure at the thin mattress and the bar pushing into my back. The light in the loft stays on for a while. I used to love novels too, but now I just wonder what they mean.

In the morning Ray takes us to Ainsworth Hot Springs. Winding north I obsess over nostalgic details, Blalock Manor, the landlocked paddle wheeler. I eat it up. Beyond Harrop's cluster we climb over Coffee Creek bluff, a narrow serpentine of road on a terrible cliff. Ray tells us about the latest accident. One night an abandoned car was found on the road. Its engine was running and the headlamps were on but with no one around. Two bodies were found on the rocky beach below, the woman with her pants around her knees. She had to pee and the man got out to see what was taking so long.

The open-air pool is unappealing and the change room is cold. Through the continuing drizzle we hurry into the steaming broth and float slowly through the cave over the mineral-smooth rock. Hot water pours from cracks and I think I might as well be at home in the shower. In the change room I can't get my clothes on fast enough. I go to the gift shop to buy a sucker hoping the sugar will jack me up.

On the drive back our conversation turns to a close encounter Ray and I had. Orange and blue lights flashed between the top of Elephant Mountain and the one opposite, across the lake. Kate is envious and my spine shivers when I see her believe. Ray and I were in different parts of town. The lights flashed five or six times. It was an authentic sighting but of what? Kate is quiet for a while and then she asks: *Was it the northern lights?* Ray takes his eyes off the road to look at me and we shrug.

On the second night, as I drift uncertainly towards sleep, a large calibre rifle bruises the night and my brain lights up like a prison break. Three shots and then a fourth squeezed off by the neighbour on the hill. He fires at the moon when he's had too much to drink and because his wife left him and because he can't find work. The valley is filled with men in their wasted prime whose reality has shriveled up smaller than the dream that brought them here, men with duplicate skills and the valley not growing enough to employ them all. Carol monitors Ray for signs of cabin fever while he keeps busy fixing the place up, adding an extra room, extending the living room onto the porch. This steady industry is reassuring, but it's solitary. And God

knows what the neighbour is firing at, if it's the sound
that fascinates him or the flash or the kick. A man alone
with a mountain will learn the art of camouflage and
travel in gulleys and leave no trace. Even the wildlife
won't see him coming. Ten shots, twelve, each one tears
the tissue of night. Then silence as he goes back to his
whisky. An inelastic calm gradually returns to the valley.

When the sun is out we sit in the yard and Katie brings
out her new camera. Carol takes the gate down and one
of the horses munches grass nearby. A stranger and a
child appear on the road at the top of the property, making their way slowly past, headed for the lake. The dogs
surface and charge out to the end of the driveway and lay
into them with their dog insults. My brother looks suspi-
cious too, watches too, and I imagine I hear a growl
forming in the back of his throat. Carol yells at the dogs
but they don't stop until the strangers have passed some
boundary only they understand. Loping back, they duck
under the trailer and return to listening sleep.

Faint sounds of Nelson skip across the lake, hammer
on bone, railcars domino. A hundred years of mining
left Groman Creek in shackles, mordant pieces of another century too heavy to cart out, culverts and an-
chors cut into rock. In awhile the dogs clamour out
again. What is it this time? Brown bear, aliens in gray
cloaks, our father's sorry ghost? Whatever, it peers at
us from behind our misunderstandings. Even the dogs
can't believe how blind we are.

Between Ray and Carol a stony silence grows. The fight they suspended for our visit keeps knocking. Ray gets a beer and tramps to the top of the pasture. He sits on a stump and smokes. I follow him and we climb to Pulpit Rock, up the gradual slope, easy compared to the steep switchback trail from the town side. Struck by the cathedral loneliness of the forest, I feel vulnerable and keep an eye on my older brother ahead of me winding through the trees. He stops to show me places where he planted pot a few summers ago. The first I've heard of it, how he hauled water from below, lovingly tended the plants, admired them like livestock. He got into an argument in the middle of Baker Street with the friend who had helped in the initial planting. Threats were shouted and Ray threw him against his truck. To keep the peace he gave him a bigger share, killing a twenty-year friendship. Pulpit Rock is smaller than I remember it, a whole lot smaller, and I think it can't be right that my memory could be so inaccurate, so wishful. We perch there on the elephant's tusk and see not a cloud in the sky and Nelson sparkling below like smashed glass, the air between us transparent and convincing.

After supper we set up the game, leaving the stir-fry leftovers on the stove and the dishes in the sink. When someone mentions TV I renounce the idea and we go through the motions, rolling the dice and interrogating each other. The dogs periodically wake up and come to stare at Carol, before they sprawl someplace else on cooler floor. The cat climbs the screen and hangs there as though clinging to glass.

What is the sixth planet from the sun? It's a question from the children's box and Kate is playing for her last wedge. She says she doesn't know and irritably won't try to guess.

I'm on my last one as well, my question being:

What football player modeled lady's pantyhose in a TV ad that was banned for being too provocative?

Joe Namath, I say. *That's hardly a sports question. I'd have thought Arts and Leisure. Wouldn't you?*

Who cares? Kate angrily sweeps the pieces off the table.

Our stupor is broken and we blink at each other in the unappealing kitchen light. I glare at her while she decides if she can lose it with me. I say something stupid sounding and start feeling sorry for myself. So much goes wrong, things nobody warns you about. You flounder badly and betray and fail and learn decades are surprisingly easy to squander. You can't let your guard down lest the sky collapse and bury you in sleep.

Driving around town we watch for real estate signs on lawns so I may indulge in my annual fantasy, with Katie and Carol along for the ride. The first house we slow down to look at is a gray stucco charmer with enough room for any sized imaginary family. But it's listed for two hundred and sixty thousand, way beyond me. A fantasy needs boundaries. The next one is a ramshackle place for eighty thousand, isolated at the top of Fell Street. On Fourth we find a nice bungalow for one-thirty. It's vacant. The realtor meets us there. From the three bedrooms upstairs Katie picks hers. The kitchen needs work, new tiles, appliances, and I could do some of the work myself.

I lie awake and inhabit the house. Katie has a brother and a couple of sisters and their mother is a composite of all my wives past and future, and all our problems are charming.

When Kate and I get back to the coast we spend the evening in front of the TV, and on the news see a story about a couple we know. Their light plane went down nearly a week ago and is lying at the bottom of a remote lake. A chequebook and a flotation device were found on the surface and the experts presumed them drowned. Next of kin were given the news, the families wrote obituaries. It struck me how quickly they resigned themselves. They sat in quiet circles with the couple's children, softening their words and feeding it to them. Then this morning the couple were spotted hiking out of the wilderness, hungry and bitter.

Isn't somebody supposed to put their foot down and refuse to give up, demand the search continue? Isn't that how it's supposed to work? Where did these expectations of loyalty come from? I keep thinking about how easily they accepted it. Why does it ring true, this lack of faith, this cowardice in our friends, and our own eagerness for loss?

After I've taken Kate to the ferry her absence injures me. That night I call and talk to Ray for a while. He tells me about a new job he expects will keep him working through spring. A project right there at Groman Creek. A house that's going to have heated floors, and an unzoned view. And even though the owners have had to resort to RRSPS to pay wages everyone is optimistic.

A month later I get a late call from Carol. Ray has had an accident but she's careful to let me know he's in stable condition before she tells me about the eight broken ribs, the punctured lung and fractured skull. He was in town having a few and she went to sleep at her usual time. She wasn't concerned. He sleeps in the cabin if he's been working on songs to all hours. Going to wake him she discovered blood all over the floor; and climbing into the loft, she found him in bed in a pool of it. When she tried to wake him all she could get was a far away, *I didn't fall.* The words were oddly conscious; his terror of being at fault transcending even this. He was incoherent as Carol and the neighbours carried him down the ladder and into the truck. The road was murder and getting him into the boat was hellish ballet. On the other side of the lake another truck, and up the hill to the hospital. The next day an ambulance takes him to Trail for a CT scan. Further x-rays reveal four crushed vertebrae. The doctors are amazed. How could he have done so much damage in a fall? And climb back into the loft? All he remembers is leaving the bar early, and setting up his tape recorder.

Winter comes and the weeks turn into months. Ray lives on morphine and sleeps most of the time. Carol goes into town every afternoon to teach. This is the best part of her long day. Lost in the needs of her students, their enthusiasm for Beethoven. She teaches them subtle vibrations of the Earth. Afterwards makes tea and stares at herself in the glazed dark. She's thinking about the amount of work it takes to live across the lake, how much more difficult it is in winter.

She buys groceries and rents a couple of movies. She unties the boat and heads out onto the lake. But a storm is waiting for her and it pushes her into a maze of pylons left over from the old wharf. The engine wails as she nurses the throttle and coaxes the lake, abuses it, hammers it, and finally steers into the open, with just the freezing rain and the whitecaps to contend with. Over the awful water, towards the dock where no light has been installed to guide her. The stars and the moon are out, and she steers by vague intuition, beacons, shades of black. Finally across, she secures the boat and covers it. Navigating the icy deck, she curses. She forgot to buy cigarettes for Ray. The truck she starts with a prayer, and cramming it into low, begins up the hill. The cranky transmission isn't one sound if you listen, but a whole chorus, each knock and groan a perfect weakness, troubling and reassuring.

CLEAN ROOM

RIVING TO THE FLATS is pretty now, under the walls of green and with the barbwire blackberry bushes coming leafy. Maples wave like children wave. Modest spring covers abandoned shells of cars and a sofa that must have died of embarrassment in the ditch. Houses at this side of Port Mann are small and ill, though their gardens are coming along. Patches of tall grass sway in every driveway, and wildflowers will always find a drainage ditch. Across the river, high on the third bank, the penitentiary sits, its black walls staggered from another century of the mind, its phlegmy cough amplified over the water. When we moved to Surrey everything was bare and gray and inconstantly wet in the throws of its dank winter.

My son tells me not to ride the brake, but my foot stays where it is to remind him whose car it is. His eyes are sunk in that gloom that hovers around him. He rolls the window down to get away from my moisturizer, which he hates the smell of. But my skin is deep not thick. It's the only salve I've got. And these are such uninspired times. I turn in on the Credit Union's white gravel parking lot and like the sound of it crunching under the tires. I give him the keys and get a fractured smile in return. Moving here has not been good for my middle son. The school system from the beginning has been trying to ruin him. It took Surrey and Mary Jane Shannon High to finish him off. Now he's stigmatized, a dropout. He slides behind the wheel and I remind him to pick me up at five.

The trailer is nice since they fixed it up with cedar siding and painted the trim a dark-eyed brown. Beside CN property it sits in a grove of cottonwoods, away from the docks and maintenance sheds, though the switching yard is splayed out behind us glinting in the sun like a mirage. In the softer light of the office Mr. O'Connor greets me, and I hang my coat on the bathroom door and sink my purse in a drawer. Scanning my desk for the end of yesterday, I see where I need to begin. It's then I realize this job is the only solid thing in my life and my legs go mushy at the thought of what I've done.

In the bathroom, I stand up to the mirror. I used to be pretty but now my face is hard to define. The joints in my hands are swollen. It could be the onset of you name it. God, what a disappointment I am. The doctor thought maybe arthritis, but he doesn't seem too bright.

From my desk I look out at the rail yard and the abundant steel glinting like licorice strips, teeth on a comb. Boxcars abacus forth and back, add up to a tomboy's dream of creosote and tar. I wanted to learn machines, to grow up with their synchronicity, to keep the whole cranky farm productive, as my father did. He could have engaged the boys, shifted them into forward, showed them how it's better to stay a step ahead of the day than a step behind it. But life is harder nowadays with everything so easy. They have their guitars and The Beatles and *my* car. Doug is supposed to be applying for work but I think he just drives around all day. The odometer tells.

Mr. O'Connor sets a coffee on my desk. His wife died a few years ago and he's near retirement. Today I have to tell him about the new job. I've been putting it off. I wish I hadn't bothered applying for it in the first place. It was more out of curiosity to see if I could. Now I feel like a traitor.

Members trickle steadily in over the day, most of them pleasant men, some I've made friends with who find excuses to come in. I've learned to distinguish between their discrete vibrations on the steps, the paunchy discontented ones and the self-taught comedians. They all have one thing in common: a natural-born entitlement over me and every woman they meet. Smelling of rust and fresh air, they're not as well educated as they think.

By lunchtime we've cashed an unusual number of personal cheques and this being payday we're worried about running out. Mr. O'Connor calls the courier but they can't make another run, and he didn't bring his car. I dial home and Doug answers in his reluctant tone. I ask him if he'll do Mr. O'Connor a favour, and he asks what it is. Doesn't he know you're supposed to say *Yes!* before you ask what it is?

He needs someone to drive him to the bank. He's going to pick up a bag of money and would feel better if he had someone along. Do you think you could do that?

How much money?

Just say yes. Don't ask a bunch of questions that make you sound lazy and stupid.

Around twenty thousand, I tell him. He doesn't need to know that but why am I unable to lie?

I make another pot of coffee and pass a dishcloth over the counter though it doesn't need it. Between the two of us we keep it spotless. While the water gurgles I stare out at the rail yard where a freight is being sectioned from smaller strands on separate stages. The cars are corralled from other lines and sent coasting with a nudge of the engine, a man on top riding the break. Flatcars brought up from the river carry machines for stripping the land. All day in the background I hear it, the cars domino in the play of their couplings. The longer segments are linked to the main string as it moves away through the grass. Boxcars are a rusty non-colour that devour light, effective camouflage to enter the realm of ghosts and whistles in the distance, warning you to stay awake or your dreams be added to its haul, harvested from the foolish and the unlucky and the dammed. In a day it will wind under the mountains and emerge on the unobstructed prairies, and how I wish I could. I'd jump off when the air smelled right of plowed wind and aspen. But the house has been hauled away and everything overgrown and with Daddy gone there's no man strong enough to take it back. Why did I accept a new job when I'm not sure it's a good idea or the right time for me?

In half an hour my diluted son and the loveliest man I know return. Mr. O'Connor goes directly to the safe in his office and I wave to my son's cigarette driving away. At three o'clock Mr. O'Connor locks the door and I get on the phone to check references. It's complicated, deciding who's worthy of trust. It seems unfair a lot of the time. I stole a dress once, put it on and walked right out of the store, and here I sit. It felt so good it scared me and I mustn't allow myself to feel that good.

The boys dish up in the kitchen and eat watching *Hogan's Heroes*. Their faces lost and at rest, insecure and arrogant, really just stretched babies. Their whiskers remind me of pubic hair and their deep voices don't make sense. Rose isn't hungry again. She's in her room with her dolls. I've never met a child who could play by herself like that. When Stan pulls in, the boys head for the basement, even though their TV show isn't over. They're alert for his sounds, the car door, his cough, and they vanish like gophers. Stan is carrying a *Vancouver Sun* and a bottle of whisky in a strangled brown bag. He drops the paper on the table and puts the bottle in the cupboard beside a nearly empty one, which he brings out. I collect the boys' supper plates, still warm from their laps, and start the dishes. Stan clinks an ice cube into his pheasant glass and pours two fingers, adding a splash of water from the tap. He flips the paper on its back and reads. After he's had a few I'll sit with him.

Why aren't the boys doing that? He asks.

I want to.

Not in the mood for debating the merits of defeat he goes to the basement, light-footed when he's on a mission, returning with Larry and Don. Their hulking flesh towers over him. It hasn't entered their consciousness how small he is, to their combined mass. Though it has apparently entered his, judging by his divide-and-conquer tactics. The boys hunch over the sink, too demoralized to think of rebellion or escape. He can't understand why they have to be told to help their mother. I couldn't explain it to him.

I pour a drink and sit down.

Mr. O'Connor was real disappointed, I tell him.

Of course he was, he says proudly.

I'm going to miss him . . . I try to explain.

He's going to miss you. It gives him satisfaction.

Stan tenses up when the music starts, the boys practicing. He unbags the new bottle. With his view of the parking lot he watches a police car pull in. Two officers get out and come to our door and Stan gets a bemused look, guessing their mission. I let them into the hall, and the boys' music rumbles up the stairs behind me. Their chords go through the floor joists and straight into the Craig's living room, terrorizing the old man, who has complained in every polite way he knows. I feel bad, but what can I do, music is all they have. No law is being broken. One of the officers says he prefers this to their being out on the street causing trouble.

They stop around ten and I finish my drink and go to bed. Stan will stay up until the bottle is three-quarters empty and then make his way upstairs to his room like a man exhausted from prayer. In the morning he'll go to work and not let on how he feels and tomorrow night he'll finish the twenty-sixer and get most of the way through another one, like tonight, like every night.

I close my office door to shut out the huffy chatter of the girls. It's a small branch, as branches go, but hectic with the business of inefficiency. My desk is covered with real work I attempt to chip away at. Buried somewhere beneath, a sign identifies me as the manager. My window to the outside overlooks the smudgy backs of boxy houses, with no greenery. And it's impossible to keep clean, with the trucks roaring up and down all day. Stan gives me a pep talk every night and every morning, I'm crawling on the freeway asking myself why. The doctor tells me I'm going through the change of life. Stan thinks I should go to somebody else, but I have enough men angry at me.

Something is wrong. I look up from my numbers in a dream. I hear a loud buzzing that I'm supposed to understand and see a blur run past my window. My staff are drunk with terror, wailing and carrying on. One bursts into my office shouting in my face that we've been held up.

That's a quaint phrase, I say, inappropriately. *A stagecoach is held up. Isn't a bank robbed?*

Luckily the girl has already flown off the handle and out of earshot of my haughty remarks. I try to rein my emotions in, to know what to do, but I can't help thinking how funny it is. I seem to have forgotten my lines. And sirens are converging on me from all over the city.

They interview us in monotones while customers squint and rattle the lock. I ask one of the girls to make a sign that says "closed" but can see my request get shredded somewhere between her ears. *Closed for police investigation* I print on letterhead and tape to the door. Finally, I've done something; I'm in control. The sign attracts even greater numbers and I feel my heart tear from the tremendous gigantic hassle of this job. After the police have done me, all I want to do is go home. How I'd love to beat that rush. I go back to my office and call home expecting Rose to answer but get Doug, which surprises me because he's supposed to be at work.

What happened? I ask.

They said I'm too slow.

Let me talk to your sister.

When Rose comes on I ask her to look up the number of my specialist.

I wrote it on the calendar, I tell her.

Where? I don't see it.

I'm short with her, *In the margin, somewhere.*

I can't see it.

Never mind. See you later.

I call my doctor's receptionist and get the number for my specialist's receptionist who, when I give her my name, says importantly, *We're to get you in as soon as possible, how is tomorrow at two?*

When the investigation is done I'm hungry and beaten and rush hour's in full swing. There's a bad taste in my mouth from too much coffee and too many cigarettes so I light another one. The receptionist's urgency flutters in my stomach and traffic crawls. It breaks out and runs headlong for a few minutes and then just as suddenly stops and I'm jolted out of my daze. I tell myself to watch the blinking road but my mind wanders to the uncomfortable places it loves to go when I'm feeling bad. It takes an hour to get as far as the Port Mann Bridge, where traffic stops altogether and I notice the gas gauge on empty, imagine running out of gas on this gritty, windy bridge. I *will* the traffic to keep moving.

I have a drink as soon as I get in and the kids crowd into the kitchen to hear about the robbery, and a shadow of fear comes over them. It hadn't occurred to me that I might have been in danger and yet it's the first thing they think of. What would they do without me?

Finding a parking space downtown takes longer than I expect. I circle the block praying for one in front of the building so I won't have to walk far. I fumble with coins and drop a quarter I don't bother to retrieve. With all the time I've wasted I'm sure to be late and I hate being late.

I lean through the heavy doors and look up and down the plastic letters. On the fourteenth floor—I notice there is no thirteenth—the doors cough me out into the smell of gauze and iodine. I'd hate to work in it. I drop painfully into a seat, ready to get up when the receptionist calls. Half an hour later she takes me down the hall to a room with no magazines where I wait another fifteen minutes. I'm furious by the time the doctor comes in but his manner is so male that my anger retreats and I smile at him competently.

Lunchtime in the auditorium, Stan is on my left, taking time out from work, looking intelligent and intense. The boys are on my right, skeptical and impatient. They didn't want to come. When Rose steps forward and does her solo, I can see how surprised they are by this talent living right under their noses. She may not be confident, but her voice is large. And my feelings are jewelry.

We have another robbery and again I'm in my office

with no clue. While the police are here I go into the bathroom and stare at myself. I'm all puffy from the cortisone the specialist has me on. He discovered something all right, not change of life or arthritis but lupus. The medicine doesn't help me feel any better and I don't like how it makes me look.

Did you see the perpetrator? Asks the young officer.

No.

Did you hear anything?

No.

He thinks I'm trying to make his life difficult.

Stan and I talk into the night. He can be so gentle with me, his voice so resonant. He should have been the singer in the family. He could have been anything he wanted, but he burned it up in his jealous war with the boys and the whisky. He thinks because he drinks in the open it makes him some kind of superior drinker, not on the sly, like weaker men. He leaves the kitchen curtain open long after being able to see past his reflection. He croons about how smart I am and how good I am at my job. I tell him that I'm going to have to quit and he agrees with me, which feels like love, and it warms me to try again.

And again we have a robbery. The police think it's the same man, but I think they're crazy. Who would be that stupid? They set up surveillance in a vacant store, rewire the tellers' buttons and install cameras. I bet the robber is having a coffee nearby, laughing at them.

Sometimes I think criminals run the world, while the rest of us play a game they've designed to keep us out of their way.

But I was wrong; he does come back for another stab at it, the same guy in the same blue ski mask. He goes to the same teller like she's an old friend, who puts money in the crumpled lunch bag he hands her and he even thanks her politely. Then he walks into the arms of rough contempt. I don't see why they have to treat him like some kind of lesser victim.

The doctor wants me to spend some time in the hospital. He says just for a few days, until things stabilize. But a few days turn into weeks and I'm forced to quit work. It's a relief not to listen to the low-class voices of those women. Stan comes every day and brings Rose every other. At first he stays for a few minutes, impatient to get on with whatever it is he's doing, but his visits get longer and quieter. I want to see more of Rose but things conspire against it and I have no say in anything. The boys are busy trying to earn a living with their rock band.

Stan stops going to work, says he's got time coming. I suppose he's discovered he works for a bunch of idiots, again. Was Stan always this lost? But I'm too blasé to pursue it. They put me in what they call a clean room, where gowns and masks are the rule and everybody's too busy to answer a simple question. Why can't I see my daughter in her graduation dress?

I was hooked up to so many machines it made me fell like a piece of land, but they've taken them away and put me in a normal room. Things are looking up, though I'm still nothing but skin and bone; and because of something they give me, my tear ducts are dry. I thought the boys were playing this weekend but maybe they were fired. They're so sad. *Cheer up*, I want to say. Their father is sharing them with me, offering them, look how valuable they have suddenly become.

FRANK'S FRIENDS

CROP DUSTERS SLIDE OVER the city, weaving and bobbing over microwave dishes and cel-phone towers, around the swaying building Mara clings to the side of. She worships it with purest insect love yet is aware of harming it in some way. The planes thunder and a mist settles. She struggles to throw off the chemical blanket and wakes beside Frank, gasping for air. His undisturbed form is not reassuring. He must be used to it.

Mara pours a drink and sits in the dark. Around her, small shapes dart and drift. Bubbles rising catch stray flakes of streetlight. Frank's fish have no colour in this absence of day, though really are brazen yellows and reds and the green she likes best. Frank thinks it odd, green a favourite colour. He tells her gold is more beautiful, and blue. She is colourblind he reminds her, that there are parts of the spectrum she can't comprehend. She will correct him: she is colour *poor*. Colourblind is what dogs are. He's right in that she can't distinguish transition shades, the in-betweens, where purple looks blue and grass is yellow ochre.

But Frank is poor in people. He can recognize rage and lust, but not the diaphanous emotions, the familiarity that accompanies anger, the irritability that swims beside love. He misses cues, misinterprets body language. He struggles along in his relationships not ever sure what's going on.

She turns on the tank lights and sits cross-legged on the dingy Oriental rug. Whatever lives in its fibres is crawling on her now. There are four tanks. Each one has a submerged building or a bubbling ship and an array of salt-water tropicals, some the size of a woman's thumb, or a baby's tongue. Fish need their sleep, according to Frank. If he were up he'd give her grief for disrupting their cycle. But Frank sleeps. Boy does he sleep. And he can't imagine the emerald greens.

Mara pulls a sweater over her housecoat, pours another glass of whiskey and grabs Frank's Players. She takes a lawn chair off the back porch from under the stalag gleam of the light in the lane. In the front yard trees block the incandescent glare and the traffic, persistent even at this hour, is barely a whisper.

She looks up at the few stars between the houses. Of all creatures man could have extinguished who would have thought the stars? The air is fresh enough and a light breeze plays with a strand of her hair. She sips the caustic liquid and feels her hatred ease, her shoulders relax. It's not that she loathes Frank per se. It's life, and poor Frank gets painted with the same wide brush. If it were not a living hell, she might love him, she doesn't know. A cat rubs her leg and with the back of her hand she pets it. How many species are cats responsible for? After their first night together, Frank told Mara it was the best night of his life, and she said, *I love you,* over and over. Only, the words had no meaning; it was the saying of them that mattered, the narcotic in the saying of them, the poison.

Lester Pearson. He pilfered it, his name, from the Nobel laureate and prime minister, thought of leaving the "B", which would have given it a dash of rock and roll. Lester B. Pearson, Johnny B. Goode. He grappled with it for months, publishing pieces of his writing under both versions, but finally decided the "B" went too far.

He says, *Did you know goldfish are greenish brown when they're in their natural habitat? They're a cyprinid fish, aren't they, like the carp, a native of eastern Asia?*

Frank is bowled over.

Goldfish are not easy to keep alive, he says.

Oh yah?

Had a dead one this morning.

No shit?

I shit you not.

Frank adores Lester, something about the way his body hangs together, loose and confident. The way he smokes cigarettes, butt between bird finger and thumb, eyes squinting through the veil of smoke. When Frank probed Mara's female intuition he was surprised she thought he was manipulative, false. Frank usually trusts her judgment, particularly when it comes to people. She understands them, sees under their skin. Her beautiful face is blade-marred, a white line from temple to chin, two surfaces that don't quite join up. The crowd she fell in with and the golf course she came from. She's wrong about Lester though, is what Frank thinks.

How much do they cost? Lester asks, of the fish, milking his enthusiasm, not wanting Frank to go soft on him. Dealers can be so touchy.

They are not cheap, I can tell you, my friend. Frank enjoys calling him friend. Frank wonders what a man can ask a man to do, socially, and not appear foolish or desperate.

You should bring your wife over, he says. *The four of us could, like, do something. Maybe take in a movie or just sit around.*

Yah, that'd be terrific, Frank. Did you say you had some hash?

Sure do. It's okay. Not fantastic. Just okay. Ten a gram.

Can I have a gram?

A gram's all you want?

All I got'sa ten.

On his way out, Lester Pearson winks at Mara like they share some secret, and she smiles weakly back to hide her mistrust. He winks at Frank too, who then regards Mara with suspicion.

Gimme a call when you feel like, you know, doing something, Frank says after him.

Right on, Frank, Lester raising an arm, not looking back.

Frank says to Mara, *I don't know why you don't like him. He's a great man. He's got a book published.*

In the years following his service in the Navy, Richard Plummer grew his hair out, braided beads into his beard, cultivated a casual walk, a lazy drawl, and a tolerance for inefficiency. Even though he had mastered this new self, his friends continued to call him Navy. He was known to put his fist through a wall when things didn't go his way. In Canada, his new friends call him Plum. And he likes that.

I worked behind a giant glass map of the world, he tells Frank. *I plotted the course in magic marker, weather, locations of hostile battle groups, suspected nukes.*

Backwards, says Frank, to show he's with him, that he understands.

It was the only skill Plummer learned in the navy, writing backwards so his commanders could read it from in front. It was a skill not marketable in the big world. He decided to become a novelist, offer his unique perspective on the greatest military power in the world.

Plummer says, *I bought some of the best dope in the world—from Africa, Greece, South America. And,* he adds, reverently, *I have seen all seven wonders, stoned.*

The last word, stretched over the chasm between them like a footbridge. *Wow,* echoes Frank.

When Plummer is over, Mara finds something to do nearby. She alphabetizes Frank's records, or she Windex's the fish tanks. When Plummer admitted his ship had carried tomahawks and nukes, she tingled all over.

Frank pushes the rug aside and from under a loose board lifts a metal box. Plummer leans over to watch. It's a treasure-trove of high-grade pot, small loaves of hashish wrapped in tin foil, and a handful of capsules, a sideline really: MDA, speed. He takes a lustful whiff.

The grass is from the Kootenays, Frank says.

Is it good?

Is it good . . .

Frank hands him a bag. Plummer nuzzles it.

How much? He asks.

I'm having some people in on Friday . . . why don't you come over?

I don't know.

I'm getting some Thai stick. We might sample it.

Concluding the transaction, Frank enjoys Plummer's formality, the hot squeeze of his large fist. He walks him out of the yard patting his shoulder. Plummer gives him a faithless grin. Mara watches from the kitchen, wondering why Frank can't see it.

Hilda Pearson, Lester's wife, is doing a social work degree. The position of anti-fairy godmother awaits her. Into people's muddy hearts she'll tramp, to take their children and blur them with other families as though for some reason that was better.

Do the rights of parents sometimes supersede the children? Hilda lectures. *If we were living a hundred years ago, and child labour was the only only means of sustaining the economy.* The others nod agreeably to whatever she says. It's in her blood.

Plummer has also brought a wife, Gloria, not his first or even his third. She's a gorgeous, jumpy mannequin, and brilliant in her way, though dieting is her central metaphor. Everything is "famished" or "insatiable" —books, museums, people. She never relaxes, and keeps an always eye on Plummer, who watches her from the back of his head.

Also here are Barry, a friend of Lester's who speaks in double and triple entendres, completely unfathomable. And Toe, an old friend of Frank's, a genuine chameleon. Mara finds him repulsive but likes having him around for how he reveals people. Standing next to Frank, he's a chair, an easy chair with fat arms and loose springs.

Frank brings out his stash. The men hover over it.

Praise be to Thailand, Frank says, removing a tightly wound green wad and handing it around. *Smell your fingers after you've held it.*

Thailand, says Lester, by way of a toast, holding up his beer.

Frank rolls three skinny joints, lights one at a time and passes them around. Sitting down to eat, Mara can see by their faces she forgot something. The chicken is overcooked and the vegetables are mush. Frank goes for it, but the others pick at it, claim to not be hungry. The men sit back in their chairs, eyes red from the weed, pretending to listen while the wives provide an endless stream of talk. If the world was coming to an end they'd build a shelter of words. But then again it is, and they have.

After supper they walk to the park. The men go on ahead tossing a Frisbee, making dashes for it into traffic, hopping fences, retrieving it from rosebushes. The wives get progressively further behind, cocooned in conversation, their imaginary skin over the brutal blood and bone world. Barry walks by himself just in front of them, listening. Not that he finds it interesting, just less threatening than the men's banter.

Blackberries grow fiercely around the edge of the park. Their Christly runners reach into pathways and grab at blood vessels and new clothes. The men spread out on the grass and throw the disk in a widening circle. The women parachute to the grass on their blanket.

Lester shows off. He chucks a curve that sails up and around a tree to the cocky Toe, who sends it long and high. Plummer doesn't have to move from where he stands to snatch it out of the air and to heave it over to

Frank, who successfully wobbles it to Barry, who, though it was a good enough throw, misses. He lobs it wide and poorly, making Lester run after it.

Frank holds up a joint and they meet centre field. The Frisbee flies better and truer after a few tokes. Relieved that he's finally gotten the hang of it Barry launches a purely magical one that catches an up-draught and sails over Lester who runs backwards with impressive speed and agility, young as a dog. He leaps into the air and falls into the waiting blackberries.

Suspended by thorns, Lester Pearson's control wavers. The men wade in, hold branches down, trying to break them, to not hurt Lester, who as a result of their effort is swallowed deeper into the thicket. Hilda shouts useless orders from the side while Plummer takes charge and devises a simple plan, to pull. Aesthetized by anger and embarrassment Lester submits to being wrenched free, punctured and shredded. Hilda wants to call an ambulance but he screams at her not to.

Back at Frank's place she tweezers out bits of thorn and applies hydrogen peroxide, a whole bottle. Frank starts to cry. He can't stand to see suffering, to not know what to do—about Mara's agony, the world's, God's lonely hell. He usually blocks it all out but this was too much, to see a proud man stripped of his armour.

Frank gets up around ten and slouches into the kitchen. Hands in his sweat pants pockets, jiggling his manhood, he waits for the water to boil, unplugs it. He has half a bowl of cornflakes and washes a cup from the pile of dirty dishes. He gets a tea bag and washes a spoon. Opening the fridge he stares in, trying to remember something. Mara won't let him make her tea.

He stands at the window, lazily watching a police car at the end of the block. He catches a glimpse of an officer running with a rifle. He wonders if there is another hostage taking in the neighbourhood. It happened a few years ago. He spots an officer duck around the back of the house, thinks it's good the police are here to protect decent people. Where is Mara? He wants her to come have a look. The door bursts off its hinges and six bulletproof vests penetrate the room like nails into a box. Frank instinctively puts his hands up. He thinks they've made a mistake, got the wrong address. Then he's hammered to the floor before he can think another thought. His hands are bound. They move the rug and go straight for the stash. Frank can't believe his eyes. He has been betrayed.

The roof of the courthouse is glass. Looking up, you see sky, or what could be sky, beyond the dirty panes and rusting brackets. The common areas are awash with light, illuminating the pitchy lives of people with problems. Mara can spot them, the wife beater, the robber. They dress like Frank: a bad haircut and cheap summer suit. He is tugging at his lapels, hiking up his trousers, trying on different faces to make the suit look better. Frank's lawyer is a terrific dresser. He appears from a door, beckoning to Frank that it's time to go.

Frank turns to Mara, *Where are the guys?*

I don't know.

Must have got held up. In traffic.

The judge reads the briefs before him and questions the black and white of technicalities. He impatiently dismisses attempts by either council to paint Frank in the various shades of good and ill. It's Frank's first offense. There were no great sums of money in his bank accounts. There is a question of excessive force used in his apprehension. Six months less a day.

Walking home, the neighbourhood seems different to Mara, the air smells better, the sounds of traffic don't jangle her. On the bridge over False Creek she stares down at the concrete water and has the novel feeling of not wanting to jump. When she gets in, there is a message on the machine for Frank to call Barry. She pokes in the number.

This is Mara, Barry, you left a message.

How's it going?

He's in jail.

Geez.

Yah.

You handling business now, he asks, grasping at straws.

Don't be dumb, Mara says, kindly. *Wanna go for a beer?* She asks.

Barry knocks on her door half an hour later and they walk over to Darby's Pub and order a jug of draught. There is something about him that Mara likes. His tongue is clean.

She recounts the story, from the morning of the bust, through bail hearings and meetings with lawyers, up to today. She tells it as much for herself, to order it, put it on a thread. Barry questions her, filling holes in the story, looking for obscure details: what kind of shoes the judge wore, if the benches were plastic or wood.

Lester, Plummer, and Toe come in. They're in a good mood. Mara asks them:

How come you guys didn't show up?

We had something important to do, says Plummer.

Frank was expecting you there.

Yah, I feel bad about that, Lester chimes.

That's the way it goes, sometimes. Frank knows that, says Toe.

The three of them start laughing and Lester apologizes, saying, *It's this unbelievable dope we just bought.*

That is good shit, says Plummer.

That guy wasn't easy to find.

He's cautious, says Toe. *You should be glad he is.*

You found a new dealer? Barry asks.

I'll introduce you, says Toe.

So how is Frank? Asks Plummer.

Six months, Barry says.

Is that all?

Less a day.

Even better, says Lester.

Will you guys sell me a joint?

Mara orders a double scotch. She doesn't want to go home just yet. Waiting for her is the gas oven and a box of razor blades. The car is parked next to her bedroom window and the vacuum cleaner hose just reaches. She will stay here with Frank's friends for a while, six months of alone stretches out in front of her like a highway to the moon. They prattle on, always a joke, a tease, a closed door to a deeper place. They speak of Frank in solemn tones like he's some kind of hero. But it's false. When Mara leaves they'll dissect him, analyze his fall in garbled logic. To the question of who betrayed him they all shrug, innocent. She's leaning toward carbon monoxide. It thrills her. Death promises to consummate their betrothal. She pays for the drink and relaxes into it.

Barry stumbles home with her, pissed and horny. He pulls off his clothes and flops onto the covers while Mara goes to the bathroom. When she returns he's fast asleep. She is outraged. How could she let this happen? She can't meet her love like this with some loosely held together excuse for a man in her bed. She wants to scream. In a housecoat and slippers she walks around the block a couple of times making her feet sore, getting disapproving looks from a couple of men plotting the destruction of the world. She lies beside Barry and rubs her cold against his heat and touches the hair on his belly. In her arms he moves like a fetus. Even asleep he loves her larger than Frank ever could. He has something. He's a drunk because he doesn't understand it. Around him things are always breaking or being created, wondrous and musical things out of thin air, or into. And it frightens him.

When Mara asks how he's doing, Frank complains a lot but the glint in his eye tells a different story. He likes being told what to do. He follows the rules, the authorities follow the rules. They play cards, watch sports on TV, talk about their drug experiences. He reads a lot, and to hear him you'd think he was the first person to discover poetry. And when Mara asks if he's looking forward to getting out, he frowns.

He asks, *How are the guys?*
Lester Pearson has a job.
Oh yah? Doing what?
Editor of some magazine. He's miserable.
He ever ask about me?
I never see him.
What about Plum?
He left Gloria.
Geez...

He's going out with some twenty-year-old, thinking about marrying her.

He'll have to get a divorce first.

I'm sure he knows that.

Where do you hear all this if you don't see them?

There's something I need to tell you.

Uh huh?

Barry moved in.

Frank looks at her dumbly.

He's helping me take care of your fish.

He moved in?

Frank, you know I can't be alone.

Yah, I know, but Barry?

There's more to him than you know.

I kept you alive, he says, resigning himself. *I can't do that from in here.*

And he's got a knack for fish. They follow him around, if that's possible. You know they would have died if it was just me.

When you're thrown together with a bunch of guys, Frank says, *you don't need to try and impress them, they just become your friends anyway, best friends. The friends I've got in here are, well . . . Say, if you see the guys tell 'em to come see me.*

Lester and Plummer smoke a joint in the parking lot next to the Corrections Canada sign. With hands in pockets, and chewing gum, they saunter through the glass doors and step between the prongs of a metal detector. A large grey man in a uniform examines the contents of their pockets. Another uniform waves them through a door into the waiting lounge. They sit in cafeteria seats at a long wide table. Lester lights a cigarette and frets about his job. Plummer is thinking about his divorces. Like skins of an onion he peels them back, making his eyes water. Frank is led in and he takes the chair across from his friends, wearing a big grin he tries to suppress. He doesn't want to show too much emotion in case they don't feel the same.

Franky boy, where's your striped suit? I thought prisoners wore a striped suit. Lester means this as a joke.

Plummer asks, *So, how are they treating you?*

It's not like I expected, says Frank. *It's not so bad. I spend the days reading and thinking. I've met some great guys. You'd like them.*

You ever get roughed up? Plummer asks. *By the guards?*

Hell no. Most of them are good guys.

Frank notices their red eyes.

How's Mara doing? He asks.

She's . . . Lester and Plummer look at each other.

I know she's living with Barry. I told her to. She can't be left alone, not even for a day. What I mean is, how does she seem?

You mean other than depressed? Asks Plummer.

Yah, other than depressed. Frank doesn't like his tone.

The same. Depressed.

How's Barry treating her?

We don't see that much of them. Barry's a bit weird, if you hadn't noticed, says Lester.

A bit weird, laughs Plummer.

Frank is disappointed.

Cold turkey, Barry says to Mara. Spitting out the unpleasant tasting words.

You telling me you want a sandwich? She asks.

It's the only way.

Some prefer turkey hot.

You're not being serious.

Maybe I don't know what you're talking about.

Cold turkey! He says, as though being more dramatic makes it clear.

Mara notices one of Frank's fish swimming erratically. She goes in for a closer look. *You sure that's a good idea?* She asks. He takes so many different drugs: trancs, codeine, pot, booze, cigarettes, coffee.

Three days go by and the strain of withdrawal is evident on his face. He paces around the apartment, watches TV. Around noon on the fourth day, ashen and shaky, he collapses. Mara calls 911 and holds onto him. If he dies she wants to be there to catch a glimpse of handsome death. Barry slumbers, safely oblivious to the suck and flow of his chaos. From the hospital he is transferred to detox where they put him on a low dose of Valium and suggest he start smoking, until the worst is over.

Being alone for Mara is like living with someone she doesn't trust. Always yammering about how stupid she is, how sick she is, how she has no right to exist. And she's right, and that's the trouble. Mara lies on her bed and drifts in and out of sleep. She makes black tea and listens to tepid classical music. She goes to the library but takes nothing out, goes to a movie only to leave part way through. She spends frantic evenings going through the white pages looking for names of lost friends. Sometimes she finds herself staring at the blades in the medicine chest. She visits Barry and sits with him in the smoking room.

After two weeks he comes back bright-eyed and irritatingly alive. He says dumb things and wants to go to adventure movies. She misses her struggle with isolation. She was just beginning to find ways to cope, books to read, old friends returning calls. He agrees to move. When he went to detox the fish seemed to know he was coming back; but this time, seeing him drag his things out, his iron typewriter, his extra shirt, they lose hope. One at a time Mara finds the fish belly up. She scoops them out and puts them in the garden. Over their bodies she says the few lines of the Lord's Prayer she can remember.

When Frank is released he fills the apartment with a thick gloom, at a loss to know what to do, how to live. He tries to maintain institutional routines, getting up at six, having porridge and hard-boiled eggs. He runs

around the block for an hour and then retires to the
bedroom and reads. At precisely noon he has lunch and
returns immediately to his room where he reads for another hour and then has a nap. He makes a list of his
friends, his acquaintances. Betrayed by one of them he
broods over the names, all of them tainted by his suspi-
cions. Face it, they hate me, he thinks. But isn't hatred
an overripe form of love? Isn't love what betrays us all
in the end? Didn't he read that somewhere?

His head hurts. He just wants to get loaded.

Toe comes over and they go out. Running into
Lester Pearson and Plummer at Darby's Frank buys a
round of beer. He tells a few prison jokes and things
loosen up. He learns that Plummer is married again
and unable to hide his resentment of the fact; that
Lester has been fired from his job after a nervous
breakdown, and that Barry is off the wagon and isolated in some little room. They go outside to smoke a
joint then come back in for more beer. Frank enjoys
himself. It's good to be back.

So, Frank, do you know if there's any good pot around?

Yah, Frank, are you going back into business?

It hits Mara hard, grief surge, which has been coming
towards her for years. It's been years since she signed
the papers and they took the baby away. She gave in to
some obscure notion that she was too screwed up to
look after a child. The social workers urged her to
think about what motherhood would be like, how it

would curtail her freedom. But what does that mean? Is freedom emptiness? She talks to someone in the ministry and learns that until the girl reaches legal age there's no chance of contact. But it gives Mara hope to proceed, to fill out forms, and suppose.

When Frank decides to go back into business Mara finds a place of her own. They remain friends and have dinner every couple of weeks. She cruises secondhand stores for baby things, a crib, a highchair, buys paint and mixes strange bright emerald greens. Frank worries that she's becoming more eccentric, even insane. He warned her against living on her own, and it pains him to see her living in the past, fixated on irrelevant furniture.

Surrounded by his fish, and the TV on without sound, Frank takes calls from his friends.

One night Mara goes for a walk and finds herself at Barry's door, her head spinning with half-formed motives. He takes her coat and offers her a drink. That he hasn't talked to anyone in a while Mara can tell by the torrent of words that pours out of him. He enfolds her in his befuddled magic and carries her to the bed. Why does he love to be naked while she remains dressed? That she doesn't understand puzzles her. She's used to seeing people as they are. Is she losing that? She hikes up her skirt and tears aside her panties.

You still on the pill? He whispers.

Nothing to worry about, she assures him, her cold hand on his warm neck.

He sends them forth, his knights, on their quixotic journey, riding off in all directions, absurdly wrong and horribly trivial. Racing up counterfeit tubes to be overcome by mediocrity; even the mighty and the lucky can't make it past the myriad intelligent distractions and noble dead ends. Getting past the drugs and the cars, the dogs and the social workers, the furtive brilliant few arrive in unselfconscious ecstasy, wanting only to serve. Meaning isn't possible. Wasted decades are the price you pay for small knowledge. Mara begins to trust her intuition and on the tenth late day when she dabs to find no blood, she's released from her prison of freedom.

REAL FAMILY

TERRY STEPS OFF THE CURB behind the bus into heavy traffic. Forty-First is three lanes now, the westbound doubled has become a racetrack and the cars sound pissed. Indecisive, he steps back. It used to be they'd stop, chivalrous with unenforceable law. Now you take your chances and choose your seconds. He steps into the first lane and stares the next car down, which wakes up the cars behind, though several break rank and hurtle by in the middle lane.

Everything he owns jingles in his pockets, the few dollars in change and his keys from when he had a private life, the repossessed Camaro and others he can't identify, magical and useless, rinky chimes. He doesn't know why he keeps them except that they're his.

He keeps jogging for how it feels and slaps a mailbox, good to be back in the neighbourhood. If Mrs. Jensen has a room available he'll drop to his knees and thank the big warden and never complain about anything again. He turns into the alley and stops running.

Her empty trashcans are nestled in the overgrown ivy. Cement Bambi watches over the groomed garden, just where it should be, the stone dove under the stairs. The house is the same, in need of a coat of paint. He'll offer to do that and to trim the bushes, for a month's rent, or for nothing.

A lift on the stairs wasn't there before and in the carport a wheelchair ramp. Her disabilities aren't getting better. He takes the stairs three at a time remembering how it used to amuse her, and he knocks at the same time he tries the knob. He used to just walk in and plunk himself down on the chair and light up a cigarette and stare at her exquisite smile. But the door is locked and he knocks harder and pushes the button. He can hear ringing from inside and he shields his eyes to peer into the murky hall. In the carport he knocks on the basement door but there's no one to answer it.

Remembering what two of his keys are for, the skeleton for his old room and the brass one, for the outside door, which he confirms, just like true love, it clicks. Inside he knocks on the doors of the empty housekeeping rooms and looks in the fridge that's bare and not running. He goes into his room and finds the bed stripped, a faint odour of mildew in the mattress. In the dresser are sheets and blankets, in the closet hangs nothing. He wonders if having a key makes him less of an intruder. This is technically breaking his parole, he supposes. Back outside he sits on the steps and shivers in the shade.

A blue Jaguar pulls into the driveway.

Can I help you? The man driving it asks.

I came to see Mrs. Jensen.

She passed away.

Terry doesn't like his manner and wants to accuse him of lying. But he checks the impulse, hearing the voice of his social worker: *You don't need to react in every situation.* Instead he asks the man when it happened.

Three months ago.

Terry doesn't ask what she died from, because he killed her with his absence. They were close. He looked out for her; but in truth, she was the strong one. In fact, she was the strongest person he ever knew. When the police came to arrest him that first time, he reacted like a cornered animal, and they were ready for him. But Mrs. Jensen put them in their place, wielding her frailty, telling Terry to calm down and to do as they asked. He obeyed her and let them bind his hands.

I was hoping she would have a room for rent, Terry says, stupidly looking for sympathy.

The house is to be sold, the man says.

Oh . . . Can you tell me where she is, I mean, buried?

Valley View.

Where's that?

Surrey.

Terry walks away down the alley. The encounter has left him feeling hollow and like he needs to act out, to steal something. His old urges return no matter how many coping skills he learns. *Let go and let God,* whatever that means; one day at a time. It's getting dark and he's no closer to figuring out where he's going. He never considered the possibility she wouldn't be here.

He gets on a bus and stares out the window and at the reflection on the window of the inside of the bus. He watches the two things at once, the lifeless passengers perhaps watching him in the same way, and the city flying past in movie time.

Downtown he can't believe how morbid people have become, how not just the homeless are homeless and every hand lacks. Being a crook in such an indiscriminate place would have no meaning. Passing a market he pockets a banana and he goes into a restaurant for a hamburger. When the waitress is in the kitchen he leaves without paying. He floats to another part of town and steals a package of cigarettes from a table at an outdoor restaurant. He tries to distinguish between languages he can't understand. They don't know how to be Canadians. In prison at least everybody knew.

About midnight he gets off at Mackenzie and Forty-First and approaches cautiously, circling the block though there seems to be no need. No cars are in the driveway and no lights are on. He lets himself in and gets a blanket from the dresser and covers himself on the bed in his old room, though it's cold and not familiar. During his sentence he didn't think about coming back. Deliberate present was always too pushy and indifference prevented him from taking those journeys. The years he knew Mrs. Jensen were the best years, he remembers now. It's hard to believe she's dead. He can feel her soft hand on his scars. He wonders why he's not dead, his life having been such a load of shit.

By the time he met her he was already doing break and enters, when shoplifting didn't give him a charge. He tried to fence the stuff but that wasn't easy and you had to know people. He'd end up just stashing it somewhere. When he complained it was too cold in his room, Mrs. Jensen called the furnace man. She invited Terry to have a coffee and gave him a cigarette, an extra extra mild cigarette, which he teased her about. So she handed him another and he smoked two at once. They were laughing when the police showed up. In the heat vent in his room they found a stamp collection and a box of old coins.

Aloneness eats at him. He digs in his jacket for the banana he stole last night. He walks to Art's, which used to be Ruby's, and sits in one of the sagging red seats. It hasn't changed. Art comes out of the kitchen and recognizes him and smiles.

Terry, right?

Yah.

I haven't seen you around for a while.

A long while.

What can I get you?

Nothing. I'm broke. Waiting for the welfare office to open.

Want a coffee?

Can I pay you later?

Art pours him a cup and goes back to the kitchen. Terry opens the paper and reads the headlines. He turns to the classifieds but his eyes glaze over with all the small print. It's too difficult when his heart's not in it. He lights his last cigarette and stares through the smoke at grainy pictures of women selling sex. He thought prostitution was illegal. What a man wants, a hooker can't supply. He walks up to the government office. With money in his pocket he feels better. Back at Art's he orders a hamburger and pays for the coffee from this morning, which makes him feel honest. The first step down a righteous path. He forgot about these sentimental hopes and silly wishes you need to survive on the outside. He tries to read the classifieds again and can't concentrate so he goes back to the empty house.

He remembers when Mrs. Jensen had to testify. What else could she do? She visited him in jail and always brought cigarettes. He didn't know what she saw in him. Nobody else ever saw anything. She just liked people.

He wakes up to the drum roll sound of a man pissing. It reverberates through the wall; a roaring flush, and the blood-on-your-eardrums hiss of the tank refilling. Whoever it is goes upstairs into the kitchen. Terry puts on his jacket and stands at the door, but the Jaguar has him cornered. The man comes out onto the porch and down the outside stairs. Terry ducks into his room, and the outside door claps shut. The car backs out and drives slowly away down the lane.

Terry feels at home in basements, with their hedge-clipper decor and garden hoses coiled on plastic drums, more congenial than glass birds and gouty sofas. A cement floor is superior to carpeting, hard and cool. You can straighten a nail on it. The furnace divides the room. Its ducts and pipes run along the ceiling, between struts and through them. It's the Tin Man's heart. Terry dares to turn the thermostat, not for warmth but to fill the silence with its rumbling. It eases his paranoia.

When Jaguar Man was here he left the upstairs door unlocked. Terry goes into the kitchen. He sits across the counter from her black swivel chair, beside the shelf where her valued trinkets still live, small things from big friends, including one of the Garfields Terry gave her, the first one, the day he got out of jail. She was so happy with it he went out and got her more of them.

Whenever he came over she moved what she was working on to make room for pencils and paper. They started with the alphabet and it was a revelation to Terry when he started to be able to read. It meant he could take his driver's test and eventually get a car. When he got his license he drove Mrs. Jensen all around, anywhere she wanted to go. *Well, Mrs. J,* he says, embarrassed to hear his voice without her there to soak up the echo. *I would have written to you, but I didn't want to do it from prison.* He realizes that was a mistake.

His eyes fill with Dead Sea and he goes downstairs to his room. It's not his room. He has no right to be here.

He skipped classes so often the teachers forgot he existed. He spent his days in the basement quiet as a rat. Upstairs the woman drank and talked on the phone. Around 3:30 Terry would go out and come home as if he had been at school. He'd get something from the fridge and go back to the basement and turn on the TV. He daydreamed about ways of killing them. He can't even remember their names. He doesn't know why people are so fond of their memories. Mrs. Jensen helped him make a list of the orphanages and foster homes, twenty-three. Most times he lasted a few months, other times a few days.

His body aches from inactivity. He wants to break the world. He hopes the trouble in the Middle East does turn into war, a big one, involving nukes and germs. That would be satisfying, exhausting. It would help him sleep at night. He walks fast and passes Granville and keeps going, crossing Oak and Cambie, still not working up a sweat. When he gets to Main Street he feels the day begin to loosen and break up. If he could just steal something he'd sleep like a sheep. In Kingston when they slammed the iron doors the whole building boomed, random and unnerving. During the day it didn't matter, but one of them near his cell woke him three or four times a night and he had to learn to function without oblivion.

Terry's friendship with Mrs. Jensen was tested again. His new apartment was an actual suite, and he started seeing a woman in the building. She had a son who came over to watch TV and ask him all kinds of questions. Where do hot dogs come from? How does a refrigerator work? Why does Mom get so mad? Terry didn't have any answers. He'd just shrug and grin. *How am I supposed to know? What am I, a dictionary?* And a few times she went after Terry with a kind of anger he never could have imagined.

The boy slept over sometimes when she was like that. Terry would make up the floor for him. He'd be asleep in the morning when he went to work and gone by the time he got home. One time the police were waiting for him. They took pictures of the apartment. The boy's mother said he was a molester and everyone seemed to automatically believe it, except for Mrs. Jensen, though her eyes held back. The suits and careers all wanted to see him go down. They had their thumbs on the flusher like it was the most natural thing in the world. He thought he didn't stand a chance. Though Mrs. Jensen was there, nobody asked for her opinion. They were so sure of his guilt it rubbed off on Terry. *If you want me to be guilty I'm guilty,* is what he wanted to say, a lie to defend himself with, but it wouldn't work that way. He turned his brain off so he wouldn't be tempted to screw up. The judge sat back and listened to the briefcases and studied their pictures and questioned the boy. He dismissed the case and blew up, said everybody was wasting his time. Mrs. Jensen gave Terry a ride back to her place and let him sleep in the den until he got back on his feet.

Terry watches Art interacting with customers, some of them regulars he recognizes from before, knots in the same old cord, conversations that last for years. When he brings Terry's fish and chips he asks how his searches are going.

He plugs in the radio he brings down from upstairs and listens to soft rock. The last time he saw Mrs. Jensen was before he went to Toronto to see his family, his real family. He borrowed the fare from her and she warned him to not expect too much. After meeting his sister a few times she said she didn't want to see him anymore. His mother didn't want to see him at all. He should have got on the plane and come straight back west. He should have thought of Mrs. Jensen and called her. But he went to a bar and started drinking and got into a fight with some guy and nearly killed him.

At the cemetery he walks between the rows scanning for her name. The headstones are flat and recessed for the convenience of lawn mowers. The names jumble in his brain until he can't see straight and he goes to ask for help. A man looks her up and points him toward the Garden of Sacrifice. When he sees her name it's a shock. Reading her there, all that's left of her, an ordering of letters, adding up to a sound, a movement of lips. Is this what he learned to read for? It's like falling into the earth, an emptying rush of loss.

He lies face down on top of her. When she releases him, he's dazed and cold and the letters of her name are jumbled up, hard.

He wanders down Seventy-Sixth Avenue until he finds a bus stop. There he leans on the pole. Away down on the flats a train is headed out of the valley, container cars rock, steel wheels ring. Aware of his cold hands he puts them in his pockets. They're all a man ever needed, to steal with. But he would trade them for her. Even if he thought he was getting cheated, he'd take that chance.

TURN ME ON, DEAD MAN

THE MEETING IS IN THE COURTYARD of an old stone building. Around them it embraces a quadrangle of lawn with the sun just above a line of trees that make up its fourth side. Doug is angry at the sun. It feels like a bullet lodged behind his eyes. A slivery lawn chair snares him in weedy gravity and around him in a circle are seated anonymous others. Pale and discouraged they seem, like grass under a trashcan lid. Leading the discussion is a muscle man in a black T-shirt. *Heroin addicts have a superiority complex,* he says. *There's a cachet about the drug, from the movies, this tragic dimension; but don't kid yourself, withdrawal from it's like having the damn flu. Cold turkey from booze can kill you.*

Doug shields his eyes and peers at the others. They are in other countries, they watch the grass grow. It's his third day at Maple Cottage and he's starting to feel . . . brittle. The first two days were mundane. He listened to people open their stories: the flight attendant blind drunk in every major city, the doctor who writes his own prescriptions for Valium and codeine, a pharmacist who chose his profession for access to Demerol. It could be a room in any rec centre, except for the embedded stench of cigarette smoke. Doug didn't know he had a story, but one begins to appear; although water damaged, its pages clumped into whole missing decades.

From the top of the stairs Mom calls them out of bed. With a sense of urgency she hurries her sons into the living room. Have the Russians started bombing? Did Freedomites blow up city hall? No, it's on Ed Sullivan, a group called The Beatles. What's interesting is *her,* captivated by the music, and made more beautiful. When it's over she sends them back to bed with the gentle warning, *before your dad comes home.*

When the first guitar appears in the house the boys take to it like termites. When one is playing, the others lean into it, fingers itching chords, so difficult at first. Larry, the oldest, takes it with him into the world and comes back with pieces of songs, *Louie Louie* and *Gloria,* the three-note themes for *The Twilight Zone* and *Bonanza. House of the Rising Sun,* the whole song. Dougy plays until his calluses sting and the strings are eaten and smell of rust and skin.

With more experience he invents chords, beads notes onto endlessly varying rhythms. He makes the guitar talk to him. Mom comes downstairs to listen and he's flustered, caught in this intimate act. She wants him to join Don and Larry's band, but he already told her he didn't want to. She tells them they have the ability to make it big, they need only want it bad enough. She uses words like talented and famous. Exotic birds, they lighten up the basement. She says they could be as big as The Beatles and Doug shakes his head, appalled at her. *All you need is to want it bad enough,* she says. But Doug has never wanted anything badly.

At the shy band's first engagement their mother sits on the sideline with the agent woman she knows from her days in Kitsilano, who books clowns into mental institutions and magicians for parties. Their young audience slumps in housecoats and rehab slippers, and seem more amused by Blackpool Rock's innocence than in the rootless pop music they play. The name was Mom's idea, after the candy. They play *And I Love Her* and *Maxwell's Silver Hammer* and one Larry and Don wrote together. A patient asks if they know any Grand Funk. Their next engagements are at a Point Grey Rec Centre seniors' night bash and on the Kitsilano Showboat between a barbershop quartet and a very young ballerina. Mom is like a member of the band. She's their Yoko Ono.

If you play *Revolution Number 9* backwards you hear, *turn me on, dead man.* It's supposed to prove Paul McCartney is dead. They listen to everything backwards looking for missing pieces of their lives. Smoke a joint outside the basement door, sit level with the speakers to listen to the white album. Alternately sob and laugh hysterically over a bass run or a turn of phrase. The way Lennon plays chords, choppy and brutal, like a barking hound.

Mom talks Dad through the nightly practice, selling him on it, reminding him where their talent comes from. A guy with a record-making machine was in the bar the night of their engagement and he sang slowly and without accompaniment, *When You were Sweet Sixteen,* in a style like the Mills Brothers. He had a real knack, but to him it was just a novelty. Mom is on it too, over the bar chatter you can hear her saying, *Wait until our children hear this.*

After the meeting Doug folds the chairs and stacks them against the building. Inside they line up for sandwiches. A woman serves them dishwater. Whispers blare, utensils clang, the monstrous clink of cup on cup. The green tray swims. Reaching for a piece of fruit his arm begins to shake, which he finds curious. With his last presence of mind he leans on the wall thinking, *how strange.* And he's unconscious before he locates the floor.

The showers have no curtain. Bathing is a quick naked dance in a cold room. The auto-toilets roar like jet engines beneath you. Someone looks in at midnight to see if you've hanged yourself. There is no hiding anything here. Pride is scraped off at the door. Your arrogance isn't worth the price of a cigarette. Every night an AA or

NA meeting goes on upstairs with former patients returning to work their twelfth step. Your story is cur-
rency, something you trade for better luck.

Doug finds the routine comforting. The only temp-
tations are carnal. With the women patients he plays
Snakes and Ladders and *Go Fish* and they bump knees
under the table. No overwhelming decisions loom, no
thousand-dollar phone bills. They all feel it, this pause
in their madness, this perfect non-time. They would
stay if they could. Most of the counselors are ex-addicts
who did.

The old institution was cut half a century ago from a
mountain. Rumours about Riverview circulated for
years, stories at which you shook your head in disbelief,
about people who ate their hands off and others whose
brains had been replaced by gyroscopes. Now, Holly-
wood North lines one of the roads with their white
trailers, and a diesel generator feeds an artificial sun.
The architecture makes a good backdrop. And wind-
less American flags look like spilled paint.

Maple Cottage is just one floor of one building, at
this location more by an accident of red tape than any
logical connection. It's funded by softer priorities and
could vanish overnight according to the whims of government accountants. Beside it, on the slope overlooking the Fraser River, you can see the thick black walls
of the BC Pen, abandoned but not budging. Someone
new arrives every day and someone reluctantly departs,
like a seventeen-year-old boy on his second time

through. Frightened of home, of friends who wait to ambush him with their good intentions, with his sad and clairvoyant mother he drives away.

Through the Whitefoot agency Blackpool Rock has work playing weekends, and they drive hundreds of miles for six-nighters—east to Nelson, north to Prince George. They learn the grind of playing to make the rent. They are paying their dues and getting laid, feeding off their dream.

At The Big O in North Van Doug makes his way through the crowd to get a beer. Someone tugs on his sleeve and offers a seat. He declines but the man introduces himself as a record company scout and waves a glass of beer at him. He forgot his business cards at home, he tells Doug, and asks how they thought up such a great name. Doug gulps the beer. The man pours him another from his companion's jug and asks how long the group has been together. Doug tries to sound enthusiastic—in case the guy's for real—and at the same time make it clear that he's no fool, in case he's not. He's going to bring his boss to see them, he promises, and gets Doug to write down where they're playing next.

Trying to stay objective about it but being defenseless against hope, he is swept up into the terrible ache of wishing. At the Purple Pigeon he watches for them, studying everyone who comes through the door, having memorized the man's ironic posture. During breaks he wanders the crowd and stands in the parking lot to see who's pulling in. And the week after that, at an obscure club in the valley, he's still watching. And it makes him sick that wanting something bad might not be enough. But it's all he has, so he vows to want even harder.

Bruce Allen comes to catch their act along with three other bands auditioning. Blackpool Rock is on last and while the first ones rumble through their half-hour sets, their allotted twenty minutes for setting up stretching to an hour, the boys drink. The second and third bands are versions of the first, polished and simple-minded, one-note basses, clichéd solos. The boys walk down the alley and smoke a joint to even out the effects of the rum. The strategy works at other gigs in familiar clubs. The music soars, spontaneous and half improvised. But tonight it's not working. They set up in *less* than the twenty minutes, as though this was important and don't stop to catch their breath or tune their instruments. Doug's innate panic driving them they launch into *Brown Sugar*, out of tune and way too fast.

Mom is offended by their loudness. The few people at tables around her have to scream at each other to have a conversation, which she interprets as a bad thing. A strobe revolves above an empty Tuesday night dance floor. The battering sound rolls off the stage, with Don shouting: *When she strips the butler flips, the footman's eyes get crossed.* Dad is amused by the bizarre spectacle, interested in getting a drink down before they retreat. During a break Mom bullies them, insisting it's too loud, so sure she's right, appalled they won't listen.

After the death of Elvis Presley there erupts a mass yearning for Beatlemania. Blackpool Rock seizes the moment and has marching band uniforms made. Don becomes Paul, Larry George, Ringo a parade of drummers who don't stay long, and Doug makes a striking John Lennon. Even off stage he plays up the resemblance, wearing the white suit from *Abbey Road*, or a fur coat as in the rooftop concert, with the ever-present National Health glasses. The best of three Beatles acts in town, they play some of the top clubs and appear on local television. Then as quickly as it began, the fad disappears.

They change the group's name to The Boys. Larry and Don insist they stick to originals and learn some early blues. They get impatient with Doug when he talks about fame. And an unlicensed after-hours club becomes their regular gig. As usual after the set, Doug slips out the door with someone for a toke and they're joined by two hookers not dressed for December, who shimmy to keep from freezing. One of them says, *Did you hear, John Lennon was shot?*

No way, he says, thinking it's supposed to be a joke, on him.

They killed him, says her friend.

That's not possible, he states categorically, *who would kill him?*

A fan, she says.

When The Boys split up, Don and Larry move to other cities, separate cities. Doug goes on welfare and plays his old guitar, the first one, the only one he hasn't had to sell. Beading convoluted chords onto a thread he keeps losing. The frets are so worn out that tuning is impossible. It's a mournful intricacy. He keeps trying to remember something but doesn't know what. He listens to muted sounds from other parts of the house: a radio murmurs one long word, a door somewhere barks, the old woman upstairs has a conversation in a foreign language.

Materializing one day at Maple Cottage is the ugliest woman Doug has ever seen. It's an odd feeling he gets from her. He's never met a woman he wouldn't consider sleeping with. Every day she occupies the same chair and wears the same frayed denim bellbottoms and tacky blue blouse. She is carefully self-conscious, conceited and enclosed. A boyfriend visits and they wander the grounds holding hands. Handsome, until he reveals sincerely rotting teeth, he sizes up everyone in the place, looking for weakness. Overhearing conversation Doug catches references to Katherine Hepburn and a snatch of something about mistaken identity. How eerily like Katherine Hepburn she is, too, with her sympathetically imperious mouth and an imitation dainty Parkinson's.

This Katherine Hepburn is a man, formerly a man. Doug needs this pointed out. One of his friends saw it, a dewlap, the uncompleted operation. Shouldn't she be using the men's bathroom? The boyfriend has a pride of ownership over her, and Doug learns he's a prostitute. A male prostitute and a transsexual in love. He wants to laugh and then he wants to cry. What does he know? His liaisons begin and end in himself. They last for maybe a month. When she looks at Doug her eyes say, *I'm just being honest with myself,* meaning the transference of her soul to another body. And he has to grant her at least the benefit of the doubt.

The sound of seizure brings two workers to the lounge. One at each end of the quavering body of a newcomer, letting the blowout run its course. Doug sees himself and, out of respect, watches. The man sleeps, withdrawal purged from his nervous system. He's actually lucky.

Katherine Hepburn has had a cold since Spencer Tracy's last visit. Doug's friend has to point out to him that she's snorting coke in her room. Wasn't this place supposed to be sacrosanct? Otherwise what would be the point? Epochs of bullshit compress into truth, surrender. The grain of credibility he was willing to grant her, he takes back. Was her metamorphosis a bid for honesty or just another way to get off? When she gets kicked out she acts triumphant. What chance does anyone have?

He stands before the row of sinks and its bank of mirrors. It's been a long time since he stared back at himself. With scissors begged from a nurse he cuts the shoulder-length hair off.

In his room, he locates his mantra from the litter of his thoughts. He can still find it, the tangible nothing, the remembering to forget.

Slitting the cellophane with his thumbnail, Donny slides the black disk from the dilated cardboard sleeve. Static on his forearms. Mindful of prints he passes it to Dougy, who holds it between his palms, flipping it over, the halved apple, the whole apple. He lays it on the platter. He spliced a stereo cartridge onto the tone arm of their mono record player and ran over-kill wires to female guitar jacks connecting separate amplifiers on either side of the basement. The scraps and tools of its invention still clutter the floor when Mom comes down with Rose. Donny toggles the amps, dialing in a quiet hum, while Dougy sets the needle down into *Abbey Road*. With a resonant click, the groove catches and pulls it in. Bass guitar punches out and a voice thin as an axe cut surprises them into stillness. This is their first stereo. They are rapt by harmonies and instruments coming from everywhere. In each song they discover the three-dimensional space around them rearranged, opening up beneath them, inside them, from a mile away. Side A ends as though killed and the trapped needle *click clicks*. Donny gets up to turn it over. Mom glances at the stairs. The music expands and contracts with the visceral innocence of it all.

DEEPER THAN
THE WORLD

PETE STANDS ON THE PORCH, the screen door gently pushing his shoulder. Warm air from the kitchen carries past him into the unsatisfied winter. He can feel it sucking at his heat, bunching up his bones. He shouts again, *Gordon!* filling the word with his lungs, pitching it to the trees, hearing how little distance it carries. If his son were in range he'd be home already, but Pete calls to wake up the land, to make it pay attention.

He sees things in the borders of his eye, against the gray foreground of the yard, things that aren't there, yet crouch and move just the same, things located in the tunnels between the eye and the brain. The colour of light shifts as he watches, making the barn seem transparent against the forest. When the change to night is complete it vanishes, as though it weren't real to begin with. He could fire a bullet at the barn and in the morning find a hole in the wood and the slug if he probed with his knife, but somehow that doesn't prove it's there now.

He's remembering Europe, a barn like this one, just out of range of the German snipers and missed by their lazy arrogant artillerymen. Pete was ordered to destroy it for that reason, and with two incendiary canisters in his pack he loped across the open ground. It was out of range, but you never knew when some farm boy was going to decide he had something to prove.

In the resonant gloom he ran his hands over smooth timbers and rubbed with his thumb an exchange of rust and examined the composition of road apples, weighing them in his hand and crumbling them, smelling. A century of weather had filled the structure with convictions and strategies and luck and the war made it forget. It held what it could, brooding over broken casings and orphaned cranks, concealing them from the impatient world.

He returned to his superiors and told them he couldn't burn the barn, lying for the first time in his life. *There's a horse in the barn, Sirs,* he answered their inquisitive look. Aloof faces deepened and came down to his level. They dismissed him with a wave and a grunt, mystified by his perilous lie but unwilling to pursue it. Word of the animal reached everyone, including the Germans it seemed; their potshots ceased for a while, the complicated air settled down. The terrified faces of the Canadians softened into resolve, and if he squinted Pete could almost believe he was back in Saskatchewan surrounded by merely tired men. Some of them went to see it for themselves. Returning, they claimed it was sorrel or swore it was a black stallion. Their will to self-preservation was eclipsed by something deeper than the world, which took hold and forced them to stop being afraid.

A new war in Europe occupies Pete's thoughts with its fascinating inventions and arrogant mama's boys, tall with propaganda. He doesn't want to think about them, but they cross into the territory of his memory. The harder he pushes them out the fiercer they get, while he labours and while he sleeps, until he's sick of it. Bewildered by the first war, by shocking reality, another is not within his grasp. And he wouldn't leave Gordon to handle the farm by himself. And he wouldn't put himself through another homecoming. But worry over Gordon has elbowed all that aside. He asked Pete this morning to go hunting with him. So why didn't he? Stuck in the mire of his thoughts, he was mulling over this Hitler.

When Shirley complains about his wasting heat he steps further onto the porch, letting the screen door smack shut, listening to how far the sound penetrates the trees. He was sending the fragrance of berry pie to call Gordon. He ate a whole one himself once, a family legend. He was every busybody's favourite. During the years Pete was away he grew into the irregular mould of his older siblings and aunts. Without a man's teeming heart to hitch up behind, the boy cut his earth according to the whim of dragonflies. Land is only a good teacher if a father is present, not an uncle or an older brother, these men would be too fair-minded. A father's burden is injustice. A boy has to learn he can face the unacceptable world alone. Pete hates Europe for what she's always asking of him, begging him back when she's in trouble, asking him to throw himself between her and the edge of change. It's going to change if it's going to change. Who but a father can teach a boy to say no to a woman?

The rifle Gordon took with him this morning was the Ross, the gun Pete brought back from the front. The gun that deafened him, the gun he slept with cocked when he was too drunk to dream. He could fire fifteen accurate rounds a minute but he doesn't know how many men he killed. From his perch the dead seemed shy; they bowed out as though called away by a wife. How embarrassed they were.

When Pete came home, Shirley met him at Melfort station. When he lifted his arms, she stepped back. She wouldn't let him drive, even to be kind, so he rode the eighty miles home in the back, breathing through his scarf. At home, she went into the house without a word. He stood in the yard between the forest and the barn. His daughters had both gone, and his eldest son. Cities steal children. Some find prosperity while others are taken for a ride and used up. Their insides are scooped out and replaced by plastic idyls, which snow when you shake them. Pete had seen too many graveyards that looked like cities. Nothing seemed familiar except his rucksack and the Ross, dangling by its canvas strap, stock dragging on the ground. Finally Gordon was brave enough to step onto the porch to get a better look at this giant in the yard. And what strange creature was this, Pete thought, too timid to live? When he held out the gun the boy smiled.

That first day he taught him to desire the rifle. Over the months and years he took him gradually deeper, pushing as far as his fear would allow, then backing down, until the trees were used to the boy and the boy was used to the father and the father could hold him in his gaze without crushing him. They picked off flying squirrels to reinforce their knowledge of flight, and hunted fox for the sheer pleasure of death.

One time they came across a four-point buck behind a mound of earth with just its head and neck visible. Gordon said he wasn't sure of hitting it. Pete easily brought it down in a routine series of movements. But the animal stood up again. Pete liked to see evidence that he wasn't as good a marksman as he thought. Gordon nudged him. Again he adjusted gravity and distance and brought the deer down. When it stood up yet again, Pete wondered what kind of mercy should attend the surviving of two executions. He looked at Gordon, laid another cartridge in the chamber and this time aimed carelessly. Down it went, and Pete was immediately angry with himself for violating the animal's luck. When Gordon was a boy he asked Pete how many men he killed. But there was only the one he knew for sure, one who fell like a sack of grain in the snow just a few yards from him, when he charged with the second wave. He told the boy it was just the one, shrugging that he wasn't sure, sometimes allowing himself to believe. When they climbed over the rise they found four bucks in the hollow, all skillfully shot in the head. Gordon gleefully took a pair of antlers in his fists though he wept.

Pete broods, watching his breath freeze, trying to intuit what Gordon is doing, where he is at that moment; keeping a fire going, no doubt, and annoyed with himself for not paying attention to the sun. He likes to get up into the trees to extend his vision and he misreads the shadows. But the land is good with him and it won't let anything happen.

When he heads back in, Shirley asks, *Where's my son?*

He's okay, Pete says, *leave me alone.*

She is always mad at him, or maybe just mad. In the front room he tightens the glow of the lamp, and lights a Vogue, letting it burn away on the dish. Catching the pendulum, he stops the clock, tired of its pointless conversation with itself, its hopeless striving to be conscious. It does neither man nor land the slightest bit of good knowing it's seven-o-six or six thirty-two.

It's a long time until morning, and to stop himself worrying he relaxes and listens to his breathing. Experienced with patience, he could easily wait a lifetime without batting an eye. It's what separates him from all the pretty dictators who tear at tomorrow to paper the here and now. Patience, a blind man staring in a mirror, an atheist's prayer. It's what a father teaches, what the seasons learn. Patience is your only weapon against God. Pete has asked in prayer for good crops and been answered with drought. He demanded the first war be stopped only to be lured by a strange patriotic lust. And for the young German's life he offered to trade something, but God doesn't listen to dreamers. He respects the patient, and war teaches patience.

He falls asleep and wakes a few hours later with *please* deforming his lips. He's been begging and he knows he must not. He stands up and goes to look out, knowing it'll be dawn soon. Opening the crystal clock face, he rolls the hands forward guessing it's about four forty-five, then he nudges the weight. Shirley comes downstairs and he pours her a cup of coffee and they stare at each other across the table.

You're too old, she says, as though she knows him better than he knows himself and violating one of their unspoken topics, one of the things they can't hide from each other, and which they don't discuss.

What are you on about? He mocks her knowledge of him by putting her down.

When you came back from the last one, she says, *it would have been easier for me if you'd been killed.*

The hardness of her words surprises Pete, hard even for her. But it's comforting to imagine the fear behind them. She doesn't mean what she says.

I drove to Melfort and waited at the station. I was there

*two hours early so I could warn you away before you ar-
rived. You were a stranger, just looking at you made me feel
like a prostitute. You were frowning at me with such hatred. I thought you'd run away. I begged God that you'd
run away.*

He watches his wife's face, aroused by her inarticu-
late emotions.

Do you think you were alone in that? He asks, carefully.

What do you mean?

You weren't so great to come back to, he says.

She flushes, offended and hurt. He takes her
thin-skinned hand and she leans back at the same time
squeezing his fingers. One sob, one tear, and she'd love
him, desire his body. A few more words would do it.
But he lets her go and stands out in the mean air, sizing
it up, watching the barn shuck off the night, the will of
old lumber. The forest divides into details. The fields
he cleared one tree at a time appear. The sawmill boiler
is vacant as rock, the hundred pound blade blocked by
the wedge they use as a break. Old-timers used the heel
of their glove to slow the spinning fly. Shirley's father,
Robert, lost his hand. It bonded to the frozen steel and
twisted off like a chicken's head.

With a light pack and the Remington over a shoulder
he scouts for prints, but it's been two weeks since the
last snowfall. The north trail has nothing to tell him either so he decides to work his way west, past Robert's

place. Soon Shirley will make her way over, to chop wood and cook his lunch. Pete skirts the house, though he can see Robert is up and about. He would just be in the way with his bitter advice and waving his hook in Pete's face.

His plan is to follow their slaughters, to do a figure eight of the two sections, keeping his search within those limits for a start. He crosses the ice bridge over the Torch, just above the rapids, and doubles back to the fork where the White Fox River joins. Across from the house he stops to study what he built with his hands, Shirley inside busy with her terrors. He follows the White Fox south, past the artesian well that forms an ice phallus, ready to crumble under its own weight and start again. When the sun comes up there'll be sundogs and rainbows in the water dust. The unbroken snow has a thin crust that impedes him and saps his energy. The municipal road he follows north. Sometimes it feels like his land, yet it belongs to Robert, and someday will be Gordon's. Is a man supposed to own rivers and pack the air tight with his memories?

Crossing the Torch again, he turns east on the river road which he and Robert cut out of the pines, bulldozing a long wound into the prettiest part of the land. It's a road with a life of its own, impassible when it rains, stranding them every spring and fall. In the dry season it produces a fine grit that hangs in your lungs and ruins engines. It's packed snow now, which would generally be good for driving, but a recent thaw has refrozen it into ruts, axle-deep in places.

All day he threads the pale crosshatch they've woven into the land. He sees nothing to intuit his son by, no shell casings melted through the crust, no voices caught in branches. The flakes are coming heavier now, though heavy is the wrong word for it, obliterating further the familiar contours, though Pete could never be lost in this territory. The same would be true of Gordon. He'd know every lair and piece of ice age debris.

Pete remembers to abandon habit, to try and think like his son, connecting the unexpected, always turning things over to get multiple perspectives. He stands still to listen, so much ice falling on the world and making no sound. And then he's back in the war, in a crater where he lay shot and freezing. The white thunder had stopped. He was happy. A grotesque face was shaking him, a young German who had no weapon or helmet. He wanted to surrender, but Pete shot him anyway, for calling him back.

The government is talking about conscription, but they won't take Gordon at his age, not for the first couple of rounds. He wanted to enlist, to go off with his friends on the adventure his generation was born for, Pete understands that. But they sat him down and talked about common sense and economics and Robert's health and how the land would miss him. From each other they couldn't hide their true reasons for wanting him to stay.

The afternoon wears on until the trees snag the sun and he's got an hour of good light left, and he can't decide what he should do with it, keep searching or get home. Maybe he's there; maybe he's wondering if he should go back out to look for Pete. Shifting the rifle from one aching shoulder to the other he feels his confusion feeding off his exhaustion. He needs to be still for a few minutes to sort through the voices, to find a calm one. He props himself against a tall birch and closes his eyes. He slumps into his patience. Let the snow keep Gordon warm if that's all that's available. Let the thirsty drink fire, and the angry eat God. No predictions or wishes or regrets, just reality. His reeling thoughts slow down and on the screen of his eyelids he sees bruises of light, floating in three-dimensional blindness. Purple blobs, ghosts. Is perception finally fragmenting, as he always knew it would. The seasons of rock, and the wars, and every single hurt stored in the skin, every injury adding up a record of loss and betrayal, until the deeper poisons leech into your blood. At Vimy they tunneled under a cemetery and skeletal hands dangled down. They dug under the German tunnels and under their map rooms and beneath their cavernous barracks where they thought they were safe from artillery and the patient Canadians.

Pete saw things then that couldn't have been real. A man's beating heart in his hand. Farm animals on their knees praying. Is it all hallucination then, is the mind so powerful it creates all this? He jerks his head up coming out of his maze. Gordon's scarf is purple. In the colourless dusk he examines the shapes of snow, the silhouettes of deadfall, and there beside him is the twisted outline of Gordon. Sweeping snow away, Pete puts a hand under his son's coat to feel the skin. He covers him with a blanket which quickly accumulates new snow and he makes a fire. Thinking about Shirley he fires the rifle three times. Maybe she's close enough to hear.

At first light he emerges from the trees. Shirley is standing on the porch. When she spots him she stumbles across the yard to hear. Pete goes to start the truck while she fixes something for him to eat on the road and collects blankets and water and medicinal whisky. The tires break free of the ice and he pulls up to the house. He inspects the chains. He gives her a stern and gentle look to which she bows her head. He drives out of the yard and up the frozen road. Within an hour he's managed to round up another man. By noon they have Gordon and are on their way to Melfort. Shirley doesn't know all this but he told her to trust him, and she knows what that means.

The city takes their youngest child, promising to teach him to walk. He masters the braces, but what are they? Only something to humiliate, make him a lurching monster. He's better off in a self-respecting wheelchair. He cheers up and entertains everyone with amazing stunts. His arms grow strong, and his hands capable of thought. He learns to explore the workings of clocks.

Pete and Shirley go to the city to bring him home. She drives while Pete sits quietly. Her face is pretty stone, a blushing cherubim. Someday she'll stand over his grave. She drives confidently and obliviously, letting the car drift down the centre of the road as they sail over the crest. Imagine a car coming the other way. You get this feeling of freedom. You just let go.

Robert Strandquist's work has been published in numerous literary journals across the country. Strandquist earned his MFA from the University of British Columbia and has received several writing awards, including the Canadian Authors' Association Award for Poetry. He grew up in Nelson, B.C. and now lives in Vancouver where he is working on a novel.